LONDON

LOVE

LIFE

Copyright © 2025 Lora Kay

All rights reserved, including the right to reproduce this book, or portions thereof in any form. No part of this text may be reproduced, transmitted, downloaded, decompiled, reverse engineered, or stored, in any form or introduced into any information storage and retrieval system, in any form or by any means, whether electronic or mechanical without the express written permission of the author.

This is a work of fiction. Names and characters are the product of the author's imagination and any resemblance to actual persons, living or dead, is entirely coincidental.

The views expressed in this work are solely those of the author and do not necessarily reflect the views of the publisher, and the publisher hereby disclaims any responsibility for them.

ISBN: 978-1-917778-45-9

LONDON

LOVE

LIFE

A Novel by

Lora Kay

Also by Lora Kay

Darkness in the Light: short stories
A Woman
A Diary of Unfaithful Stories

*To Angel, my living guardian angel
who opened the door to
another world for me.
I hope you remain my guardian angel
and watch over me from above.*

CHAPTER I

LONDON

*'A journey of a thousand miles
begins with a single step …'*
Lao Tzu

England. Majestic, rainy and now my home, since making the biggest decision of my life.

My mother says that the happiest day of her life was the first time I cried – the day I was born. A close second, she claims, was the arrival of my sister, a new member in what seemed like a perfect, happy family: proud parents and their two lovely daughters. It sounds ideal, normal. Only after I grew up did I realise that, nowadays, 'normal' is something rare, a blessing even, while everything else is exactly what we call it – 'everyday monotony'.

Not everything was easy growing up, and I know it wasn't meant to be; life usually makes us what we have to be, not what we want to be. There's always a reason, even if, at first, it's hard to recognise …

*'Fate is so obvious, and we are so blind
that even when
it leads us by hand, we do not notice it.
We see everything clear,
when it becomes a past …'*
proverb

... I wiped the last table, sitting in its usual uneven line alongside the other tables in front of the bar. It always annoyed me how the customers would shuffle them and then leave chaos behind. Putting them back was never easy; the tables were heavy, and my hands weren't exactly strong, but I didn't complain. I was just grateful to have a job at all. Anyway, this only happened on sunny days, which were rare in this city.

I tried to slow down my frantic pace. The fresh air felt good, soothing the grumpy mood born from hours spent working in a cramped kitchen and dashing back and forth around the café. It wasn't fair on Lucy, though; the poor girl was now sweating behind the counter, handling the long queue that had formed since I'd been sent outside. But I knew she had her own ways of sneaking off for breaks – stealing a few quiet moments for a cigarette here and there.

A large raindrop splashed onto the table in front of me. I looked up, surprised to see clouds gathering overhead, though I shouldn't have been. It was typical English weather. My thoughts drifted quickly to the day I made the big decision ...

> *'You can't give your life more days,*
> *but you can give your days more life'*
> Chinese Wisdom

... Huddled comfortably on my chair, I was gazing out the window. Elbows resting on the ledge, chin in my hands, I'd felt a rare sense of tranquillity, not disturbed by my mother walking in the room, nor my sister, or even the dog. Outside, a gentle summer rain had just begun, each drop tapping softly against the glass. Something was missing in my life. The raindrops seemed to fit so perfectly with the world, each drop a part of nature's rhythm. *Tap-tap.* Yet I felt separate, as if I didn't belong to my surroundings. My life felt like a movie I was watching from the sidelines, never truly a part of it. Something essential was missing – there was a gap I could never quite fill. *Tap-tap.*

Sometimes, I'd wonder if – perhaps – I was just different. Everyone around me seemed content to walk the same path – school, university, work, marriage. It was a well-structured path, but I felt empty when I thought about it. My future had always appeared blurred, no matter how hard I tried to envision it, as if *my* path lay somewhere else entirely. Perhaps that was why I could never see my future clearly; meanwhile, the view through the window, at that exact moment, was something sharp, lucid. That rainy afternoon, something in me shifted. I realised the answer had been right in front of me all along; I just needed to follow the rain. And the rain led me to England, my beginning ...

'Unrequited love loves for two'
Arkady Davidovich

... I stacked the chairs under the shed as best I could, trying to keep them dry as the rain increased.

'Hey, Patty.' The sudden sound of my name made me jump – I nearly dropped the ashtray I was holding.

I turned to see David, a colleague who'd been at the café much longer than me. He was tall, and athletic, and his blond hair and bright blue eyes gave him a friendly, and even charming, look. I'd noticed his gaze lingering on me ever since I started working there, though I hadn't paid it much attention – I was too focused on adjusting to my new life. Lucy suspected David's interest in me, but I refused to consider it; I didn't see him that way.

'Leave it. I'll finish up here,' he said with a smile. 'Lucy could use a hand inside with the crowd of caffeine addicts.'

And there he was, ready to save me from struggling with the heavy tables and chairs in the rain, offering to switch places so I could take over the not-so-heavy work. I appreciated it, whether it was a small, romantically-charged, gentleman's gesture or just one colleague helping another – it didn't matter at that moment. But I secretly hoped it was the second.

'Thank you,' I replied, a bit awkwardly, as his eyes lingered just a second too long.

He gave a little nod and I hurried inside, avoiding his gaze. Behind the bar, things were in full swing; orders were coming about as fast as the rain.

'Looks like someone can't bear to see you struggle,' Lucy whispered, passing by with a full tray in hand, eyes gleaming with mischief. I shot her a frown, which only seemed to encourage her because she then winked at me.

Another day had passed. Sometimes I wondered how I was managing the exhaustion that came with this new life – work, home, and work again, with little time for anything else. But somehow, I found the strength to keep going, reminding myself that perhaps my limits were greater than I realised. As my father liked to say, *'The human being is full of surprises.'* I missed my family. Now they were so far away, at a distance I could only cross in my thoughts when the lonely moments came.

Lucy and I were the last to leave, locking up the bar behind us, but she had the day off tomorrow – free to sleep and relax as much as she wanted. I'd soon be back for another round.

'Well, that's it for today,' Lucy announced with a theatrical sigh as a smile full of cheek creeped across her face. 'Another day of proof that David's love runs deep …'

I rolled my eyes. 'Get some rest tomorrow, Lucy,' I said as I began walking by her. 'And maybe get those ideas out of your head,' I called, sending a kiss through the air.

As I got further away, I could still hear her laughing. I found myself smiling; she might drive me crazy with her endless theories about David, but she was like a sister to me – something precious beyond value when one lives in another world.

The rain had stopped, but I tilted my head to the sky, wondering if it would return overnight – I had a uniform to wash. The clouds were beginning to part, and the colours of the sunset were peeking through. As I watched, a plane crossed overhead, dragging brushstroke trails across the sky. I smiled, reminded of my own journey on the day I left home for England …

*'The courage is not the absence of fear,
but the triumph over it …'*
Nelson Mandela

… The big day had arrived. My suitcase was packed, but my stomach was a knot of nerves. The choice to leave had been mine, and my family supported it completely – so why was I still so anxious? *Everything would be fine,* I kept repeating to myself, but it wasn't working. I was terrified.

The airport was huge and overwhelming. Thousands of people, some making tearful goodbyes, others in joyful reunion. I clung to my family as long as I could, not wanting to turn away from the arms hugging me tightly or the tears sending me off. My family suffered from the long separation of unknown length, but they gave me the support I needed to get to the airport with my big suitcase. Released like a bird that was about to learn to fly, I took my way in life.

'We'll talk again in a few hours,' I promised, forcing a cheerful voice to mask my fear. 'I'll call as soon as I land.' I had to sound strong, even if I didn't feel it. I couldn't be weak – not now. This was my chance, my dream, and it was just beginning.

I slowed my steps, watching other travellers to figure out where to go and what to do. Doing this alone made it harder – if only I had a companion. Airports looked so glamorous in movies, as if flying abroad was always the start of a great adventure. For me, it felt like anything but that.

At the security check, I removed my shoes and belt and placed them in the tray. When I passed through the metal detector without any beeps, I exhaled with relief and hurried to collect my belongings so I could check my gate. Luckily, I overheard a couple next to me who happened to be flying to the same place and I decided to stick near them, grateful for the chance to keep from getting lost.

Nervously, I watched the minutes slip away, and soon I found myself in the massive queue at Gate 11. In front of me stood a guy about my age, he had a backpack slung over his shoulder and looked to be focusing on the book he was reading. From what I could tell, he was handsome, but at that moment, I wasn't in the mood to check out some cute stranger. He looked comfortable and calm, like someone who'd been through this a hundred times.

Meanwhile, I was a bundle of nerves, wide-eyed and trembling.

Aboard the plane, the cabin crew greeted us with warm smiles. I was astounded by the plane's size and how something so massive could even fly – intuition told me it weighed a bit more than a feather. My seat was next to the window, and I vowed not to miss a second of this journey, even if it meant not blinking. Small drops of rain began to fall on the tarmac, and I smiled. It felt like a sign – a welcome to the country I was flying to, a lucky omen.

'Excuse me, but I think you're in my seat,' a man's voice said, breaking me out of the comfort of my thoughts. I turned to see the guy from the queue, now looking at his ticket instead of his book and appearing slightly confused. He was, in fact, really good looking: green eyes and brownish messy hair.

'Oh, um … I thought …' I stammered, quickly pulling out my own ticket to check. 'No, 33A is mine.' I felt some confidence come back to me.

I was pretty sure I wasn't wrong; it had taken me a while before I finally managed to find my seat with the assistance of one of the cabin crew. The good-looking guy with green eyes glanced at his ticket again and chuckled.

'You're right. My mistake! I'm in the seat just in front of you. Sorry about that.'

'No problem,' I replied, speaking slightly quicker than I'd intended, and turned back to the window.

A few minutes later, the passengers had all more or less settled into their places, and the guy turned to face me with a smile.

'First time flying?'

I wasn't prepared for someone to take interest in me at the moment; I was fully absorbed in my own world, where radical changes were happening, and it was difficult to concentrate on anything else. But something in his eyes felt comfortable, and it was nice to feel like maybe I wasn't entirely alone in this adventure.

'Yes,' I admitted, unable to hide it. 'Is it that obvious?'

'Just a little,' he said – it felt comforting. Then, as the cabin crew finished their safety instructions, he added, 'Don't be afraid. I can hold your hand until we take off. I'm Chris, by the way.'

Caught off guard, I hesitated at first, but upon a second thought, I decided to be impulsive and do something I wouldn't usually do. I stretched my hand to his. 'I'm Patricia. And ... thanks,' I replied quietly, letting him hold my hand. His grip was steady and warm, and I found myself blushing, hoping it wouldn't show.

As the plane picked up speed, I instinctively squeezed his hand. Soon, we left the ground, and the view from my window left me speechless. I had never imagined that there would be such beauty – the Earth from another angle, from where the birds could see it. It was impossible not to appreciate our home when you looked at it from that angle. We rose above the summer rain clouds, and before us, the vast blue revealed itself. Here, far from the chaos that we, people, created for ourselves down on earth, only beauty and tranquillity reigned. Almost like Heaven.

Eventually, I remembered I was still holding Chris's hand and pulled away, now feeling shy. But he didn't seem fazed and began chatting with me. We nearly spoke through the entire flight, for which I was grateful to him. I learned he was a university student near London, heading back after a term break.

As I looked around, I noticed that everyone else seemed calm, but I could see the tension in their eyes – none of us would relax completely until we landed. Up there, we felt small and fragile, as though reminded of our vulnerability in the face of nature's power. In moments like these, people turned to prayer, even if they weren't great believers. How easy it was to forget this feeling once we touched down and returned to our lives, where we felt invincible and in control.

'Get ready for landing; please fasten your seatbelts!' the pilot announced, and the crew began their final checks.

'Well, your first flight's almost over,' Chris said, grinning.

'It wasn't scary at all,' I replied, rolling my eyes. 'I feel so silly now.'

'Everyone's first flight feels like that. You'll see, it only gets easier. You did great!' Chris gave me a playful wink, and I smiled back, feeling braver.

'Only experienced things are truly understood ...'
Thomas Aquinas

... I decided not to take the bus home. It was only a few stops, and the cool air this evening seemed perfect for a refreshing walk. It was odd how my thoughts wandered back to that first trip and Chris, wondering where he might be now. It had been months since that day, and of course, I had no idea. I remembered how he'd offered to help with my suitcase, even though he didn't need to wait for any luggage. Like a true gentleman, he stayed with me. In the end, he wished me luck on my life adventure and hugged me as though we were lifelong friends. Then, just like that, he left.

I couldn't say I was disappointed, on the contrary – I was surprised. Chris didn't even ask for my phone number or social media to stay in touch. He'd helped me, purely out of kindness, and simply moved on. Thinking back, I realised people like him were rare.

Finally, I arrived home. *Home, sweet home.* Except, did it really feel that way? All I had was a small room in a shared house. It wasn't exactly spacious, but truth be told, I didn't need more. After a long, exhausting day, this tiny cubicle of a room reminded me I was on my own – no parents, no sister, not even a boyfriend. If I'd had a larger, more comfortable, place it might have felt emptier, so for now, the room was enough.

I sank onto the not-so-soft bed with the sigh of someone who was more than tired. *Another day.* It hit me then that it had been half a year since I'd moved to London. I felt I should probably celebrate – I'd made it! I hadn't given up. A feeling of pride began growing in my chest. Yet, it was still too early for real celebration. The plan was to settle here; there was still a long way to go, and things could turn at any moment. But I had to admit – I'd been lucky.

> **'Fate chooses the challenges we face,**
> **but we choose how to face them.'**
> proverb

A few days after I arrived in London, I moved into a room that a distant friend of my family had helped me find. Then it was time to start building my future – I went job hunting.

I walked, uncertain, along the busy streets, almost scared. *A tourist walks more boldly,* I thought, but then again, I wasn't on vacation – I would live here from this moment on. I kept my eyes peeled for recruitment ads, and the first one I saw in a small shop gave me a burst of excitement. *Here we go. This isn't so hard after all.* It took me over ten minutes to work up the courage to go inside, and in less than half that time, I was back outside, disappointed. Apparently, they'd 'just filled' the position.

'One failed attempt doesn't mean anything,' I told myself. I choked back tears and kept going. The day was long and exhausting, with little success. That evening, I went back to my small room feeling down and longing to talk to my family. I didn't feel like cooking in the shared kitchen, something I'd have to get used to eventually. It would take some time for me to get used to the whole sharing situation, but that was a problem that would solve itself with time – I had another, far bigger, problem for the time being.

The next day mirrored the first – more disappointment. The third one began similarly. This time, however, I made my way into the city on foot instead of by bus, thinking that it was a good way to get to know the neighbourhood. When it came to approaching places, I was already more confident and courageous, mainly because I felt a bit over it from the constant rejections, so shyness didn't bother me anymore. I even checked places without posted job adverts – still nothing.

By midday, I needed a break and headed into a large, bustling café. The place was busy, maybe because of its location on the main street. The poor staff no doubt went mad at peak hours. I queued up for coffee, and when it was finally my turn to order, I caught the two girls behind the counter exchanging a brief comment. The place was loud – anyone in my position probably would have missed what they said – but fortunately, I was observant.

'Seriously, if we don't hire someone soon, I'm quitting!' muttered a girl with fiery red hair, pulled back in a messy ponytail. A few stray hairs framed her face, which was strikingly pale. A smattering of piercings and tattoos completed her style.

'Tell me about it,' her colleague replied, and then she looked at me. 'What'll it be for you?'

I found myself blinking, almost in disbelief as their words sunk in. Were they looking for staff? This could be my chance!

'Oh great, another one who can't decide,' the red-haired girl spat under her breath, no doubt thinking I couldn't hear, or maybe she was simply fed up.

'An espresso and a croissant please, and also … I'm looking for a job.' I finally let it out.

Both girls looked at me, mouths half-open in surprise, as if they hadn't expected anyone to overhear. The red-haired girl quickly broke the silence.

'Find a table and wait. I'll let the manager know.' She was still speaking as she disappeared behind the bar before I could even say 'thank you'. She seemed more eager than I was. I guessed they were afraid I might disappear as quickly as I'd showed up.

Taking my coffee and croissant, I found an empty table and had barely taken a bite when I sensed someone nearby. I turned and saw the red-haired girl again, now standing beside me.

'No time for formalities,' she said. 'Let's see what you can do for a few hours, and if it works out, you're hired. Simple.' She tossed an apron onto my lap with a wink.

I swallowed quickly, stood up and adjusted the apron. Was this really happening?

'Wonderful. I'm Patricia, by the way.' I felt I should introduce myself; they could surely afford at least that much formality, I guessed.

'Lucy,' she smiled, motioning for me to follow her.

'There must be love in life – a great love for a lifetime, that justifies the unreasonable fits of despair we are subjected to.'
Albert Camus

… As the months passed imperceptibly, work kept me busy. Lucy quickly became my closest friend, and we often laughed together, remembering my first day. I had worked hard, and I was appreciated for it, which allowed me to finally settle into my new life and establish connections with others. With friends around, I no longer felt alone. I could describe what I was feeling back then with one word: satisfaction. After years of wandering in search of myself and my path, I had finally found the answer – London. It was something I never would have guessed. I didn't have a prestigious job, nor were my family or old friends with me, but here, I felt a sense of freedom and tranquillity I had never known.

But even as things began to fall into place, something was always missing – then and now: love. Despite the frantic pursuit and need of it, I had never truly experienced it. My relationships were a cycle of beginnings and separations, lies and tears, promises and broken hopes … same end, different man. They'd been a bitter experience somewhere between great expectations and reality. Nevertheless, it was my belief that love, the greatest power of all, was what moved the world. And though I'd faced countless disappointments, I kept my heart open and hopeful. I'd left my comfort zone to live in this big city, and I didn't regret it, not even during nostalgic nights filled with tears. Anything was possible in any moment, and by that same logic, I felt there had to be a chance to meet *him*, the other half of my soul. I imagined he was out there somewhere, looking for me, too. My unshakable romanticism made me patient in anticipation of the moment when my heart would skip a beat. Until then, I'd simply wait.

> ***'A human lives 75% with his fantasy and only 25% with facts – that's his power and his weakness.'***
> E.M.Remarque

… It was the end of the working day. My team's energy buzzed with excitement, like a group of college students ready for a night out, but I didn't want to take part. Not that my colleagues didn't try to force me into it, but I was utterly drained. Right then, all I dreamed of was a hot shower, a hint of creamy lotion on my freshly washed skin, and finally, my bed. This thought made me almost as happy as my colleagues looked, but for a very different reason.

The plan was to go out after closing. Jokes and teasers accompanied each handling of a dirty dish, each throwing of a wet cloth for wiping tables. Feeling their excitement was making me happy as well, but I had already announced my firm decision to go home after work. It seemed, however, that no one believed me, in spite of the fact that I stated my intentions, perfectly clear, not only twice but three times.

David was busy doing the daily account when Lucy crept up behind me and, in a flash, jumped on me.

'Lucy! You scared me to death!' I shouted, but it only made her laugh harder, and David glanced over his shoulder to see what was going on.

'Are you ready?' she asked, still catching her breath.

'Yes, I'm ready ... to go home.' I stressed my answer, not sure why she was asking when she certainly already knew my plan. Her grin told me she had other ideas.

Lucy rolled her eyes and snorted impatiently. Before I knew it, she had grabbed my hand and was dragging me to the bathroom. I felt sure I was going to wake up the following day with bruises that perfectly matched her fingerprints. She locked the door and started digging into her oversized pink backpack, which held an astonishing array of things she probably didn't need.

'What are you ...?' I began looking for an explanation for her totally illogical actions, but again, faster than me, she interrupted.

'Listen Patty, you might not have noticed, but our dear David has a thing for you – he's more excited about tonight than any woman I've seen getting ready for a night out,' she declared, already loosening my hair and trying to style it.

I frowned, wondering when all this with David had started. I had some memory of him being very nice to me several times, and I'd caught him looking at me a few times, sure, but nothing that deserved any amount of fuss. He wasn't my type, and I'd never considered him that way, but here was Lucy, assuring me it was obvious to everyone but me.

'Lucy,' I sighed, as she carefully applied bright red lipstick to my lips. I waited for her to finish, not wanting to walk out looking like a clown. 'Honestly, I hadn't noticed, and I'm happy to keep it that way.'

I glanced in the mirror, catching a glimpse of my reflection – it looked back, exhausted, on the edge of giving up against Lucy, and wearing makeup that didn't suit me. She wasn't listening to me and began busying herself with my blouse, adjusting it to reveal more skin. The modest cut didn't allow the view she was trying to achieve, but the designer hadn't anticipated Lucy's determination.

'There. All ready!' she exclaimed with a smile, as if she hadn't heard a word I'd said. 'Don't frown! Be good, and let's see what happens.' She winked.

'Nothing will happen!' I said, a bit sharper than intended, but Lucy only turned to me with her puppy-dog eyes.

'Come on, Patty,' she said gently. 'Life isn't just about work. When was the last time you went out?'

Somewhere between her pleading voice and her pitiful expression, I gave in. I figured a little fun couldn't hurt – I could sleep in tomorrow. Lucy jumped joyfully at my 'Okay', and I had to remind her that we were still in the bathroom. As soon as we got out, we found everyone else already waiting outside. Their joyful laughter and jokes spread all across the street. Someone taking pictures, another with a cigarette in hand. They handed me a small plastic cup with a drink. Judging by the smell, it was alcoholic, but well mixed with juice. I smiled to myself – it was true, it'd been ages since I'd let myself have fun.

We began walking in the direction of some bar nearby, according to Lucy. We went on until we realised we'd been walking for thirty minutes, which according to Lucy's calculations was impossible. This brought on a new wave of laughter and jokes. Perhaps it was the exhaustion mixing with the alcohol that was warming up my throat so nicely and relaxing my tense muscles, or the euphoria itself of having fun for what felt like the first time since my arrival in London, but time felt as though it had, somehow, stopped. At that moment, there was nothing but me and my new friends in a moment of happiness that would be sealed in my memories.

So we lost the way to the bar we were heading for originally, or we just forgot where we were going, and somehow we found ourselves in a small park. We sat, not very comfortably, on a bench and continued our fun. When the walking had stopped, I could properly feel the sharp piercing air – perhaps the only thing I couldn't quite get used to in this country was the cold.

'Here, take my scarf,' David offered, suddenly sitting beside me. I was sure that I'd sat as far away from him as possible, but clearly this wasn't an obstacle for him. He'd moved and approached me while the others were too busy telling jokes. Or perhaps they were even pretending not to notice in order to give us some privacy.

'Oh, that is very nice Dave, but won't you get cold?' I wanted to make sure I wasn't about to be the cause of some eventual flu.

'Don't worry. I grew up here – I'm used to the weather. You're shaking,' he insisted, concerned.

'Thank you.' It was one of those scarves I liked very much, practically a blanket, and within seconds, the goosebumps faded. His gesture of kindness felt familiar, and Lucy's earlier words echoed in my mind.

'I've wanted to see you outside of work for a while,' he began, his voice warm with excitement. 'I'm glad you finally joined us tonight.'

The sun had already set. I couldn't see his eyes well, but this was also because I was avoiding his gaze. David was a good guy, for as much as I knew, charming and handsome, too. Why this wasn't enough for me to accept his sweet insistence, I didn't know, but at that exact moment, I wanted to be wiped from the face of the Earth, to disappear and avoid the need to answer.

'Oh, Dave,' I said, trying to sound casual, 'it just takes time to adapt. I've only been here five months, and I've been working hard. But tonight is fun, and we should do this more often!'

As soon as I said this, I realised these words carried a promise that would give him hope, but in vain – the last thing I wanted for anyone. The smile on his face couldn't stretch more. I'd had the effect I was hoping to sneak by.

'Yes, that's what I've been saying! It's great we all finally did it.'

We exchanged a few more words, and just as I was running out of small talk, Lucy saved me, announcing it was late and some of us had an early shift. I couldn't have been more grateful, even though she didn't realise what she'd done for me. We all went in different directions and promised that we'd repeat the fun night again soon …

> *'Whoever seeks a friend without flaws*
> *will remain alone …'*
> Karakalpak proverb

I lay in my bed, eyelids heavy with exhaustion, but my mind was still awake. I thought about the past year in London and the situation with David. After our first night out, many more followed. Somehow, it had become a tradition – every Friday after work, we'd go out to catch up.

I thought it was a good way for the team to get closer and build up trust. A friendly environment could make even the heaviest work feel less like an obligation. But I hadn't anticipated that this little 'tradition' would fuel David's interest in me. Colleagues came and went, and new faces joined our team, but my hope that he'd set his sights on one of them faded with each passing day. He felt more comfortable with the time and would already boldly wrap his arm around my shoulders, stand close when we went out as a team, and send 'friendly' texts to check on me. I couldn't pretend to be blind to it anymore. I couldn't pretend this didn't bother me, because he was already making his intentions perfectly clear.

David's presence felt both familiar and, at times, slightly suffocating. I valued his friendship, yet there was an underlying sense of pressure – an expectation that I would eventually let him into my life in a way I didn't want to. In moments of vulnerability, I almost considered accepting the affection, security and comfort he offered, but a quiet voice inside me resisted. If I made the choice to let it happen, I already knew how it would end – I wouldn't find happiness, and certainly, I wouldn't find love. The little voice reminded me that the easiest path isn't always the right one. I don't know how I knew this so instinctively when I lacked experience, yet the lesson felt imprinted on my soul, as if I'd already lived it once before. It felt as though something was waiting for me to decide, and this time, it was urging me to choose differently.

The friendly circle I'd found myself in by such unbelievable luck gave me the comfort and peace I needed, especially here in this big city where I was so alone. I didn't want to mislead David, and I hoped he'd pick up on my 'just friends' signals. I had a lot of trouble being harsh – it wasn't in my nature. And so, we arrived at the moment I'd hoped would never come …

> ***'Friendship can end in love,***
> ***love in friendship rarely …'***
> Charles Caleb Colton

After another Friday out, after everyone had gone on their way, David insisted on walking me home. The idea terrified me, and I tried to assure him it wasn't necessary and that I could do it perfectly well by myself, just like any other day, but he was insistent, wanting to 'make sure I was safe'. I guessed the beers he had earlier had given him courage. He walked with me, despite my attempts to make him turn back. In front of my house, just as I hoped to end the evening with a polite goodbye, I felt his hand catch mine, and I was forced to face him. I could see the battle in his eyes – courage and boldness against fear and insecurity. I frowned and opened my mouth to tell him not to do this, that we were better off without these complications, but I was cut short by a sudden kiss. The courage in him had prevailed. For the brief moment when his lips touched mine, I felt … nothing. There was no magic, no butterflies in the chest, no connecting of souls …

I pulled away immediately, and he, visibly embarrassed, apologised. I believe in that moment he realised that I'd never given him a reason to think something like a kiss was available. He left nearly at a run, and I stood there, imagining that nothing would be the same from then on.

Could I blame him? Of course not. Sometimes, in search of the right person, we meet many others who give a pale likeness to the sweet feeling of love, and we follow it. It's easy for a person to be deceived, and then comes the bitterness of realisation; the journey continues, but not hand-in-hand with the person we thought was for us. It had happened to me a fair number of times. This time, though, I wasn't the one disappointed.

For a short while after, David avoided me. I knew why, and I wanted to reassure him that we could still be friends. But I decided to let him come back on his own terms. To my surprise, he resumed the old routine quickly, pretending nothing had happened. He laughed, joked, and casually wrapped his arm around my shoulders again – it was like nothing had changed. I was confused, but I left things as they were, praying that the kiss would never repeat again …

> *'Sometimes I'll come when you're asleep,*
> *An unexpected visitor.*
> *Don't leave me outside in the street.*
> *Don't bar the door!*
> *I'll enter quietly, softly I'll sit.*
> *And gaze upon you in the dark.*
> *Then when my eyes have gazed their fill,*
> *I'll kiss you and depart.'*
> Nikola Vaptsarov

… Somewhere between my chaotic thoughts, I must have drifted to sleep. I couldn't otherwise explain how I found myself staring into a pair of warm brown eyes – intense, mesmerising eyes belonging to a man whose face was both visible and not. But I knew one thing – he wasn't anyone I'd ever met, yet his presence felt natural, magnetic. I wanted to reach out, to touch him, but I couldn't. He kept looking at me as if he wanted to tell me something, but I heard only silence and the beat of a heart.

I woke up suddenly and felt dizzy from the rush back to reality. Breathing heavily, I sat up and sipped some water, glancing at the clock. It was just past midnight. Oddly, I'd only been asleep for a few minutes, though it felt like hours. I got up to splash water on my face and then curled back into bed, hugging my pillow. The shadows in my room slowly came into focus: the picture of my family on the cabinet, the little chair by the wardrobe.

My dreams have always been strange, inexplicably so, and even a little frightening. When I was younger, I used to be fascinated by what they could mean, but soon after, I realised there wasn't much certainty in their transcription, so I decided to leave it to my imagination. But there were moments, just like the one I'd just experienced, in which a certain dream would shake me with its reality and feeling. And then the question always came back: what are these visions – what do they mean?

I'd read all sorts of articles, wondering whether dreams were echoes of emotions, projections of suppressed feelings, or perhaps even … memories of past lives. Whatever the answer, my dreams were different, standing out in ways I couldn't quite explain. Maybe there was something wrong with me. I almost laughed at myself. I rubbed my eyes, yawned, and settled down to sleep again.

'Intuition is the whisper of the spirit …'
Peter Dimkov

I woke up feeling far from rested but forced myself out of bed. Lucy hadn't felt well and had asked me to cover her shift, making it a long day for me. I sighed and checked my phone, and without any surprise, I saw messages from my mom, who was still getting the hang of technology because of me. Skimming her texts, I chuckled. She was asking if I'd 'found a boyfriend' yet, or if there was a 'cute colleague'. I shoved my phone aside. The last thing I wanted to think about was David, who'd latched onto the idea of 'us'.

I had my habits, one was never leaving the house without a good breakfast and a strong coffee, even if it meant waking up earlier. I wasn't one to rush out the door, and like everyone, I had my vanities – I always made sure to emphasise my almond-shaped eyes and full lips.

When I finally arrived at work, the day took off at full speed – orders, cleaning, more orders, my feet aching from constant running up and down. When it came time for my break, I put on my headphones, closed my eyes, and let my favourite song have its effect on me. I must have been more exhausted than I'd realised because I managed to drift off. There they were again – those brown eyes, watching me intensely, radiating warmth, calling for me to find them: *'Soon my love, soon ...'*

I jumped awake, almost shouting, and found David standing nearby, looking at me with obvious concern. Realising I hadn't heard him because my headphones were still in, I quickly pulled them out, feeling awkward with him standing so close.

'Hey, Patty, are you all right?' he asked, his expression saying plenty. I could only imagine how I looked – napping during my break, hair messy and eyes barely open.

'Sorry, Dave. I must be tired,' I said, trying to smooth my hair.

'No worries, I just wanted to check on you. You've been working a lot ... If you need anything, you know you can count on me, right?' He looked at me with those big blue eyes, his expression softening into a hopeful smile – he'd gladly be my knight in shining armour.

'Thanks, but you know I'm just working a lot because it keeps me from going crazy at home. I'm fine, really, just tired,' I said, trying to create a little more comfortable distance between us. 'But I appreciate you looking out for me.'

I smiled at him and literally ran to the kitchen before he could respond. David seemed a little down for the rest of the day, probably thinking I was a bit crazy, which I didn't mind – anything that made him forget about the idea of 'us'. Truth be told, I *was* feeling a little crazy. I couldn't shake the strange dream for the rest of the shift, and it hung off my shoulder the whole way home. Odd as it was to dream it twice in twenty-four hours, I felt a flutter of excitement in my chest, reassuring me that whatever had drawn me to this country was part of a journey, one I was meant to be on. Something was waiting for me …

'You cannot insure yourself out of the love fire'
Edith Piaf

More than a month had passed since the dreams started. Today, I woke up feeling refreshed, thanks to a dream that was more beautiful than any I could remember having. I hadn't seen his eyes this time, but I felt his hands – gentle, comforting, holding me. It felt like safety, like home. For a moment, I wished I could drift back to sleep and let it continue …

When I finally looked at the clock, I nearly jumped. Without realising, I'd fallen asleep again and lost half an hour. I was late and already knew that today would be the worst. I calculated what I could skip – breakfast was out, hair would have to be done on the bus, and maybe some mascara if I could find a seat. I threw everything into my bag and rushed out the door.

I barely caught the bus, breathing a sigh of relief as I stepped on, but there was no space to make myself look more presentable. *Oh well*, I thought, *not like I have anyone to impress.*

After three stops, I hopped off and continued the last five minutes on foot. As I hurried, texting Lucy to advise her that I was running late, I trusted my feet to guide me since I knew the route by heart. But as life was about to remind me, expectations and plans were about as fragile as the surface of a puddle.

A sudden collision sent me off balance, and I would've fallen if whomever it was I'd bumped hadn't steadied me.

'What's wrong with you?' someone shouted. They sounded angry.

Recovering, I looked up to see a guy looking back. He must've been leaning against the street pole, phone in hand just like me, before I ran into him.

'I'm so sorry,' I said uneasily.

But my embarrassment was only growing – he was, without a doubt, handsome, and I must've been staring at him like an idiot. But to my surprise, his irritation softened, and a smile even began tugging at the corners of his mouth as he looked at me.

'If I hadn't been here, would you have run straight into that pole?' he asked, raising an eyebrow in amusement.

Completely caught off guard, I stammered, visualising myself hitting the pole and ending up on the curb. 'I … um … probably,' I admitted, blushing. 'I'm just really late.'

'Well, thank goodness I was here then,' he replied, his smile widening. His gaze was steady, his eyes a deep brown, like coffee with a little cream, or cocoa – warm. I was yelling at myself to get to the restaurant, but my feet were glued to the spot – I couldn't bring myself to walk away.

'Yes, I … Thank you. And I'm sorry, but I really have to go!' I blurted out and dashed across the street, quickly entering the café. *Just my luck*, I thought miserably. Not only had I run into someone on my worst day, but he happened to be a charmer, and I'd ended the situation running away like some skittish rabbit, literally running away. I felt like such an idiot!

I hurried to the staff room, my mind whirling. My hands trembled as I struggled to tie my apron. I couldn't stop my heart from racing or quiet the butterflies fluttering in my chest.

'Hey, is everything okay?' a voice interrupted. I jumped and held back a nervous yelp. It was David.

'Sorry, didn't mean to scare you, just to …' He looked me up and down, taking in my frazzled state.

'It's fine, Dave. I'm just late,' I replied a bit sharply, brushing past him, aware my tone probably startled him. But his hovering presence was too much at that moment; I needed space. I grabbed a tray of clean dishes and headed to the bar.

'Patty, I saw your text and—' Lucy was cut off by a sudden crash. The tray had slipped from my hands, shattering glasses and scattering cutlery across the floor.

For a second, everyone stared, then returned to their business. But I was completely unable to move. At the front of the queue, waiting to order, was *him* – the guy from the street. He was watching me, a small, amused smile playing on his lips. I tried analysing the situation, thinking that he must have seen me entering the café and followed me. *Followed?* I was clearly feeling a bit too self-confident. He wouldn't have any reason for interest in me – especially not today. He probably just happened to be a customer.

'What's wrong with you?' Lucy hissed.

That question seemed to have been chasing me lately; something must have been happening with me because everyone kept asking. After quickly gathering the broken pieces of dishes, I pulled her aside and told her about my morning disaster. She burst out laughing.

'Finally! Someone who can make our Patty's heart race!' she teased. 'Poor David will suffer, but I'll be thrilled if it means you're happy.'

'Lucy, keep it down!' I whispered, glancing around. 'Besides, he's a total stranger. Nothing's going to happen!'

'Honey, how long he will be a stranger depends only on you. And to be honest, I have a good sense for romantic stories, and I tell you, here and now, that this is one of them!' She winked at me, as she was wont to do, and headed for the bar.

Taking a deep breath, I steadied myself and prepared to face whatever came next. But he was gone. *Of course he's gone*, I thought, feeling a wave of disappointment. I'd missed my chance, twice in a row, but it was probably for good.

The rest of my shift dragged on, my mind too preoccupied to make sense of much around me. When the day had finally ended, I grabbed my jacket and made a swift exit, calling a quick goodbye as I left, eager to escape to my room, away from prying questions. I needed to be alone and had a desperate need for chocolate.

I stopped at the supermarket for sweeties; today would be a day I didn't think about calories. Once home, I sat on my bed with my laptop, determined to lose myself in my favourite movie, a bag of chocolates, and a hope for a better end to a not-so-great day.

*'Eventually soulmates meet,
for they have the same hiding place.'*
Robert Brault

I didn't dream that night, or at least I had no memory of it in the morning. With no need to wake up early, I had plenty of time to spoil myself a little. I decided to straighten my normally-curly hair, and somewhere between styling my hair, singing along to my playlist, and applying some makeup, I received a text. I glanced to see if it was important, but it was just Lucy, so I turned back to the mirror. My phone buzzed again. I was sure she was teasing me about last night – about the whole incident with the charming stranger and the spectacular tray dropping. Her amusement over it all seemed endless. Regardless, I decided to check the message just in case:

Honey, you have to come a little early today.
I'm sorry for the last-minute notice,
but it's important. Kisses

I sighed, looking at myself in the mirror. At least I had time to look decent today. Not that it mattered for work, and certainly not because I expected to cross paths with a handsome stranger again, but for once, I felt genuinely good in my own skin.

OK, I'm coming

I replied and went to get dressed.

As I headed out, I wondered what was so urgent. Maybe someone had called in sick, or it was just an unexpectedly busy day. It didn't really matter; tomorrow was my day off, and an extra hour of work today wouldn't kill me.

When I finally arrived, the bar was calm. Normally, we joked in such moments, calling it the 'calm before the storm' – soon enough, we'd have a crowd of customers all at once.

Lucy crossed my way, practically appearing out of nowhere, her expression one of pure mischief. I knew that look all too well.

'Oh, you look so good today! Just *perfect* for the occasion …' Her eyes were like that of a sweet devil as she glanced towards the back of the bar.

I stared at her, confused. 'What are you talking about?' I asked, but she just repeated her gesture towards the bar, beyond it.

Following her gaze, I finally spotted him. There, at the farthest table, sat the stranger from yesterday. Alone, smiling in my direction. I whipped back around to Lucy, whose grin had grown smug.

'What have you done!?' My teeth were clenched.

'Nothing! I swear,' she said, her innocence entirely unconvincing. 'He came by asking for you, and I told him when your shift starts. He was disappointed he couldn't reach you to invite you for coffee. Naturally, as a good friend of yours, I told him I could arrange for you to come in early.'

She looked so pleased with herself; meanwhile, I felt an oncoming wave of panic. What now? Was I supposed to just sit and have coffee with the man who, at this very moment, was responsible for my sweaty palms and the fact I could actually hear my own heartbeat throbbing in my ears?

'And lucky for you, you got yourself all dolled up! Now go! He's watching us,' she urged, nudging me forward. She was right. Standing there like a fool, delaying the inevitable, was pointless – I could argue with her later.

'I'll kill you later!' I muttered, heading for the table.

'You mean you'll thank me later,' Lucy corrected. Her smile was so wide I could see every tooth she had in that red head of hers.

Relax, relax, relax, I repeated to myself as I approached him, trying to calm my nerves. He looked up at me – he looked so calm, cheerful even.

I cleared my throat and pulled out the empty chair, sitting down. 'Hi,' I said, unsure of what to expect. If Lucy was telling the truth, he was there to see me. He actually wanted to get to know me. Yet instead of exciting me, this fact only made me feel even more nervous.

'Hello,' he replied, still smiling. Why was he so amused? I hadn't the slightest idea of how to proceed, so I was relieved when he spoke first, sparing me the pressure of coming up with an opening line.

'You look a bit different today,' he said. It felt like he was studying me.

'Maybe it's my hair; it's usually curly.' How he'd noticed when yesterday's meeting was so brief, I had no idea. He was observant, that was for sure, though this thought was hardly comforting as I didn't want him remembering how I'd looked when we first met.

'So you got yourself ready just for me today?' he said. His smile was still so easy. Where was my easy smile, my calm?

I could hardly believe his audacity. Did he really think I'd do that for him? It was more than ridiculous, and the fact he was interpreting it in this way was less than what I would have liked. Perhaps his smile was more self-satisfied than charming, and I still couldn't decide if he was mocking me or simply smug. My face grew hot, and my words came out fast and sharp.

'Not at all! I didn't even know you'd be here … eh …' I realised I didn't know his name yet.

'Martin,' he filled in the gap.

'… Martin. This is a complete surprise to me, and my appearance has absolutely nothing to do with you. This is simply how I look – yesterday, I was just in a rush.'

I was quite pleased with my answer, and I thought I'd finally gained the upper hand.

'Shame,' he shrugged, 'I thought your natural curls suited you better.'

I stared, open-mouthed. Had he just implied I looked worse today? Apparently, his good looks didn't come with a matching personality.

'I didn't mean to offend you, Patricia. You're beautiful either way,' he said, softening. For a moment, his words left me silent, caught between feeling flattered and annoyed. Also, how did he know my name?

'How do you know my name?' I came right out with it.

'Your colleague was kind enough to tell me,' he replied. I felt slightly foolish for not putting that together.

'Perhaps a bit too kind, considering she arranged this meeting without my knowledge,' I said, adding a pointed edge.

He looked apologetic for a moment. I felt satisfied to finally make him feel uncomfortable.

'Sorry about that.' For a moment, his eyebrows frowned. 'To be honest, I'd have done it myself if I had your number.'

His smile returned, disarming me yet again. Martin here knew exactly the effect he had on people – especially women. But I was different, and he'd soon realise that.

'Well, of course you don't have it. The opposite would be odd,' I said, knowing it wasn't the most natural way to phrase it, but I was frazzled, and when I was frazzled, English felt harder to pin down in my head. 'After all, self-respecting women don't give their numbers to men they just met on the street.'

No matter how hard I tried, I couldn't deny the magnetic pull I felt towards him. As much as I wanted to give him a hard time, I felt a thrill sparking inside me. I could deceive anyone else – Lucy, and Martin even – by keeping up my indifferent front, but I couldn't deceive myself. At that very moment, I felt something like love, and I could feel myself running towards it.

'Your colleague looks a little upset,' Martin said, nodding behind me. 'Sorry, is he your boyfriend? Have I imposed?' I turned to see David vanish behind the kitchen door. Fantastic – the last thing I needed was for my coworkers to witness this.

'He's not my boyfriend. We're just good friends,' I replied, feeling things getting more and more complicated.

'Then perhaps it's best I let you get back to work,' Martin said. My heart sank; the end had come far too quickly, 'And since I don't have your number to make a real date, how about I come by to pick you up when you're done for the day?'

This time I was unable to restrain my smile. There was no reason to be stubborn anymore.

'I'm off at eight.'

'I'll be here.'

When he left, I went to the staff room to get ready for my shift. My hands were trembling again. Would this happen every time I saw him? Lucy had been waiting to attack me with questions. I tried to give her a brief rundown, though it was hard to keep a straight face. David passed by us not saying a word. There was notable anger on his face, maybe pain, maybe disappointment. Lucy made a bored face and commented that he'd cry his eyes out, but it wasn't funny to me. I'd never wanted to hurt anyone, and seeing the effect this had on him was difficult to bear. Still, I couldn't change how I felt. I hadn't mislead him – I'd made it clear I didn't want more than his friendship. Of course, I knew he didn't see it that way, and that in his eyes I might have been a monster.

The rest of the day passed in a blur. When I finished my shift, Martin was there as he'd promised. Smiling, leaning casually against the street pole, he waited for me. And so, it all began…

> ***'Love each other dearly always. There is scarcely anything else in the world but that: to love one another.'***
> Victor Hugo

* * *

> ***'Love is the only passion that does not recognise either past or future'***
> Honore de Balzac

'Patty, leave that box – it's too heavy …' Martin called out, noticing my determined struggle just in time.

'Everything is under control … I've got it … I can handle …' I insisted breathlessly, but my arms gave out, and the heavy cardboard box loudly dropped to the floor. 'At least it wasn't fragile,' I sighed, brushing away the stubborn strand of hair stuck to my sweaty face. I glared at the box, silently willing it not to betray me so easily again.

'I don't know if I'll ever get used to your stubbornness,' he laughed, gathering up the scattered items for me.

I shot him a dramatised frown. Martin often mentioned this side of me, and he wasn't alone in noticing it. My closest friends saw it too, but I hadn't decided if I should be proud of it, as something that often brings drive and victory, or see it as a flaw. With Martin beside me, it was true that I didn't always need to be handling everything on my own.

Getting used to him in my life hadn't been hard. The thought still made me blush, even after a year together. He had changed everything; I hardly recognised myself. Was this the magic of love that everyone was always talking about?

I used to believe that one's personality built up in the early years, layering over time but rarely changing at its core. That a strong will could modify traits, but the roots always stayed the same. I even argued that people couldn't experience deep transformation. And yet, here I was, unrecognisable even to myself. Life has a way of proving us wrong, reminding us how much we still have to learn. Luckily for me, my lesson was sweet, and I wouldn't mind learning it over and over again. So yes, I realised that people can indeed change, all because of love, the greatest, most powerful feeling of all.

'Love is a glory affordable for everyone'
Lev Landau

I hung up the phone, ending an hour-long conversation with my mother. I was so excited, and she was, of course, the first person I had to tell. She shared my happiness, but as always, couldn't help giving advice – this was a mother's job. 'The great passionate fire of love could burn you in the end!' she warned gently. But how could I explain in words the connection I had with Martin? It felt beyond human understanding, something only the universe could comprehend because it was a part of it.

I called Lucy next. She was my only close friend here, far from home. However, London was feeling more and more like a new home, and that thought raised the excitement in me, a tsunami pulling the waters back, threatening to sweep my world. Perhaps my mother didn't use the right term – instead of 'burn', maybe I would sink. In any case, there was no hope for me. Some would say I was 'blessed with what would destroy me' while others would claim I was 'exalted to the ultimate happiness'.

'Hey Patty! What's new?' Lucy's cheerful voice greeted me.

'You will not believe it!' I barely managed to keep my voice level. There was a squeak in the back of my throat threatening to shoot out with every word. I felt moments away from bursting with joy.

'Don't keep me in suspense! Spill it!' she urged, not knowing whether my news was good or bad.

'Martin and I are moving in together!' I said – I practically sang it.

'Honestly ... that's not exactly shocking,' she laughed. Her reaction surprised me – I expected excitement and congratulations.

'What do you mean?'

'Oh, Patty, come on! It's no surprise. Everyone who knows you was expecting this. You two are so connected – it's like one of those fairy tales, you know? *And they lived happily ever after* is exactly what comes to mind.'

I smiled at the comparison. I knew our bond was unique, but I hadn't realised it was so obvious to others.

'I hope so,' I replied, my voice coming out soft, hooking momentarily on all those pesky uncertainties, the *what ifs* and *shoulds* that tend to float around big decisions.

'Now tell me everything,' she said, her excitement beginning to show. 'When did you decide? Did he ask you ...?'

Questions poured out of her, and I felt my face flush with the memory ...

***'In love there are only two things –
bodies and words'***
Joyce Oats

* * *

***'The pleasures of the body often depend more on
the way the soul touches, not the hand'***
proverb

    I expected Martin to arrive at any moment. I'd set up my little room perfectly for the occasion. I'd unfolded the small table to create space between the bed and wardrobe: wine glasses and plates decorated with salad surrounding the main dish. Tonight called for a romantic touch, so I lit a candle. The truth was, I was eager to use the candle holder I'd bought recently, a replica in the ancient Roman style from a local antique shop. Its charm had drawn me in instantly, and I walked out with a smile and my new purchase.

    I loved these little moments – dinner with Martin, then curling up together on the tiny single bed, talking until late. Space was tight, but waking up beside him, even on the cramped bed, was worth every ache in my neck and back.

    There was a knock at the door, and I rushed to open it.

    'Hi,' I said.

    'Hello,' he replied.

    A smile spread itself across my face.

    He leaned in and kissed the corner of my mouth – I loved when he did that.

    We settled down for dinner, and he reached across the table to take my hand, lifting it to his lips. It was his quiet way of thanking me for the food I'd prepared, and as usual, I felt my face heat up. His effect on me was as strong as ever. Delicate, gentle, respectful, and affectionate, and at the same time restrained in showing emotions – Martin was like medicine to me, an invigorating tonic, and my destruction, for my life and afterwards!

As we talked about our day, I noticed he seemed distracted, as though his thoughts were elsewhere. A flash of unease struck me where I usually felt butterflies. Was he okay? Tired maybe? Or was I, as usual, imagining things? He took another sip of wine and then stared into it, tracing the rim of the glass with his finger. I fell silent in anticipation, mirroring his gaze as he gave his glass a little swirl.

Suddenly, he stopped, his fingers steady on the stem as he looked up to meet my eyes. 'I think it's time we found a more comfortable place … for both of us.'

I was breathless from surprise. It's not that I hadn't thought about it – the idea had actually been a regularly intrusive thought of mine lately – but I didn't know if it was the right time to bring it up, whether he would agree or not. To hear my thought come out of his mouth simply knocked me for a minute.

How good it would be to live together. Instead of *'see you tomorrow'*, we'd just say *'good night'*, falling asleep beside each other. I knew my answer. I felt like a schoolgirl who knew the response to the teacher's question; I wanted to jump with a raised hand. Yes, a thousand times YES! But I'd probably embarrass myself with such a reaction, so instead I cleared my throat.

'I think that would be the most logical thing to do,' I whispered, holding back the excitement that was ready to burst.

Martin nodded, not taking his eyes off mine, and I noticed how his lips curved into a quiet smile. I couldn't hold back any longer; I leaned across the table and kissed him. A short and tender touch on the lips – it was the best way I could describe how I felt. He loved me!

Slowly, he rose, wrapping his arms around me. This time, like every other, it was much more than just a physical merging of two bodies. It was as if our souls were one; it went beyond any ordinary orgasm …

'Love without respect does not go far and does not rise high. It is an angel with one wing.'
A. Duma – son

* * *

'During times of universal deceit, telling the truth becomes a revolutionary act.'
George Orwell

* * *

'The biggest lie is to deceive love. To rest on one's shoulder,
while desiring someone else's. To kiss with eyes closed, in which
the reflection of another image burns.
Your silence lies more than words …'
Blaga Dimitrova

It was better that Lucy couldn't see me through the phone. I was blushing with the memory of Martin's proposal to live together, replaying it vividly in my mind. I'd conveniently skipped over the most intimate part – some things just felt too personal to share.

'Well, have you started looking for an apartment yet?' she asked, curiosity evident in her voice.

'Yes. Actually, we've already found one! I'm so excited, but there is a lot to do to make it feel like home. I'll have to talk to Nian about some time off to settle in.'

'Already!?' her voice turned playfully reproachful. 'When did all of this happen?'

I bit my lips, bracing for her reaction. 'A week ago …'

'And you're only telling me now? Someday you'll get married, and I'll find out after the wedding! You're too private, Patty,' Lucy muttered with the affectionate exasperation only she could pull off. Her words hit a nerve, though, a bit unexpected – a little grain of sand on the bottom of my foot that I couldn't seem to brush away, but I felt it when I took a step. It was my latest intrusive thought: could I picture myself in that white dress one day? The idea scared me. Or rather, the idea of wanting it – I didn't want to mess up what I already had?

'Anyway,' Lucy said, pulling me from my reverie, 'since you're so happily in love and cutting down your work hours to enjoy life with your boyfriend, you've been missing all the juicy work gossip.'

'For instance?' I asked, a bit embarrassed to admit how oblivious I'd been. After those early days in London when I barely knew what a day off was, now I was enjoying the city with Martin by my side.

'Well, for starters … about David,' she teased, drawing out the words for dramatic effect.

'Dave?' I repeated, surprised. It was true I hadn't paid much attention to him lately. After all, once Martin and I got serious, Dave's initial low-spirit mood seemed to evaporate, replaced by his usual easy-going self. It felt like everything had returned to normal, and I was relieved. David was a friend, and I'd hoped our friendship would continue, free of the awkward potential.

'Yes, *our* Dave,' Lucy emphasised, making it clear I'd missed something significant. 'You remember the new girl, Carol? Turns out they had a thing going – officially together and everything!'

'Wow!' Carol had been with us a month and was already dating Dave? That was fast.

'Save the surprise,' Lucy laughed, sounding smug, 'because unlike you and your fairy-tale romance, theirs is already over.'

'Really?' Now I was truly surprised. This was either a whirlwind romance done wrong or plain bad luck.

'Again, I'll ask you to hold your surprise,' Lucy continued, amused by my reaction. 'Apparently, a few days ago, Carol showed up to work red-eyed from crying, heartbroken. Turns out, while Dave was in the shower, she stumbled upon his phone, and she discovered that he'd had a flippin' serious girlfriend for months.'

Lucy finished with a dramatic flourish, and I stood there speechless. The news felt like a slap, one that stung more for what it revealed about Dave.

'Now you can say "wow",' Lucy added.

I couldn't find words, shocked and disgusted by what I'd heard.

'Can you believe it? You could've been wrapped around his little finger, too. Who would've thought that behind that innocent face and sweetness was someone so … untrustworthy.'

The conversation didn't last much longer, but after I hung up, I lay on my bed, lost in thought. How had I missed this side of David? Beneath the good looks and manners lay something much less appealing – selfishness and indifference to others. My gut had saved me this time, yet how many others, like poor Carol, hadn't been so lucky?

Honour, dignity, honesty and love used to mean something. Now they felt hollow; there was hypocrisy behind the smile, carelessness behind the word 'love', and lack of honour behind the promises that were meant to be kept. Was this something new, or had people always been this way?

> **'In the arithmetic of love, one plus one equals everything,
> and two minus one equals nothing.'**
> Mignon McLaughlin

It took two days for Martin and I to move into our new place that we now called home. It wasn't particularly large, but it didn't need to be. We had each other, and that was what mattered. I was ecstatic to leave my cramped room behind and share my days with him.

The living room opened up into the kitchen, with a small hallway leading to our bedroom and the bathroom. I was putting books on the shelf when I felt Martin's arms wrap around me. We were both a mess from the unpacking, but there was always time for pleasant little moments. I smiled.

'Look what I found after you dropped the box.' He held out an old photo album.

'My album! I know just the place for it.'

I took the album and set it on the shelf, where it fit perfectly. Then, on second thought, I took it back down and pulled Martin to the couch.

He laughed as I made him sit. 'What's this?'

I patted the cover of the album. 'Creating traditions. Once a year, we'll sit down and look through all our captured memories.'

'You know, that doesn't sound half bad.' He flipped open the cover to a photo of us on a rare sunny day in the park. I was holding a bag of nuts I'd been feeding to squirrels.

'Look, you had longer hair then,' I noticed, running my fingers through his now-shorter cut.

'And you almost fainted when that duck came up to you for a hazelnut!' he teased. We laughed as we flipped through more pages, each photo sparking memories of happy moments caught and preserved through the lens of the camera. One of my favourite photos was from our trip …

'Everything is small to love. It has the happiness, but it wants heaven, it has heaven, but it wants sky.'
Victor Hugo

It was a rainy afternoon. With little else to do in such weather, we sat on my single bed in my little room playing cards. Suddenly he paused, and I could actually see an idea spreading across his face.

'What …?' I asked, unable to guess.

'I think I just solved our bad weather problem.' He narrowed his eyes, knowingly leaving me in suspense.

I frowned. 'I don't understand …'

'If the sun won't come to us, let's go to the sun.'

'Are you suggesting space travel?'

A reflexive laugh bounced out of him and around the room. 'I'm suggesting a vacation, regular travel.

I actually shouted as I jumped to hug him. We spent the rest of the afternoon choosing where we'd go and buying tickets. My heart was racing and a smile was glued to my face the entire time – I felt like I'd drunk three coffees in one go. Martin had to remind me that we still had a month until our flight. A whole month! I knew I didn't have a choice in the matter of waiting, but I didn't feel like I could do it.

Fortunately, the month flew by, and I soon had my little suitcase neatly packed and secured with a padlock. I was dressed in summer clothes, which didn't pair well with the brisk wind and gathering rain clouds. Still, in just a few hours, I would be somewhere with nothing but bright blue sky and fiery sun overhead – I couldn't resist dressing for the occasion. My phone buzzed with a text. I didn't even look before grabbing my suitcase and heading for the door, but then I paused to check, just in case it wasn't Martin:

Have a wonderful time, sweetie! Collect some sunshine for me and send photos. Kisses.

'Ah, Lucy.' I returned to my bed in anticipation. My phone buzzed once more:

I'm downstairs, waiting for you.

As I reached the front door, I saw the taxi parked outside. Martin got out with his usual charming smile and took my suitcase to place it beside his in the trunk.

'Ready?' he asked as we settled in the car.

'I've been ready ever since we bought the tickets.'

'Well then, off to Havana!' he officially announced.

This flight felt completely different from my first. I remembered Chris and how kind he was to me on that trip, assuring me that my next trip would be less scary and more exciting. He was right. My worries had been replaced with anticipation, and yet, one thing was the same – just like before, I was holding someone's hand. This time it was the hand of the man I loved and had found where I'd least expected. Everything felt crystal clear to me now – the thread that connected us all along had brought me to London. I'd often wondered what force had called me there, what mystery had led me to take such a leap. The answer was right there, holding my hand, watching the view through the plane window.

'You must be the change you want to see in the world.'
Gandhi

My father once told me that each person is born with a path set before them, though we rarely recognise it. Instead, we begin to live the way we can, facing crossroads and dilemmas, making choices – some right, some wrong. But when we trust our inner voice and make the right choices, the obstacles seem to fade away. Sadly, this process remains unclear to most people – they call it 'luck'. The truth is that the universe is working in every moment, for someone to go in the right direction, even if they do so unconsciously.

When I was young, I often questioned my father's philosophy. Was he right, or could there be other answers? Which principles would guide my own life? Over time, I saw the wisdom in his words, with the help of which I built my own perception of the world that distinguished me from most people …

'Fate rarely obstructs the path of the clever man.'
Seneca

I burst through the door of our flat with such energy that Martin nearly dropped his cup of tea.

'You won't believe it!' I practically shouted, loud enough for the entire building to hear. I tossed my bag to the floor, kicked off my heels, and with a movement somewhere between jumping and dancing, I approached Martin. My face, stretched in the widest smile, almost ached. He was staring at me with wide eyes, but he was calm – it was obvious I didn't have bad news.

'What happened?' he asked.

'Well ... someone just got a new job! They hired me!' I nearly knocked him over as I flung myself at him, laughing and hugging him so tightly that his words came out in a strangled murmur.

'Great news ... tell me everything.'

When I finally released him, I wiped a tear from my cheek.

'But ... you're crying?'

'Yes,' I sighed, 'I'm so happy ... and I'm not used to things going so smoothly. I'm almost afraid that it's all too perfect and could disappear.'

Martin wrapped me in his arms, my head resting against his chest, and I listened to the calming rhythm of his heartbeat.

'Don't worry. Life knows what it's doing. If you're given something good, it's because you deserve it.' He pulled back, smiling at me. 'And you, my love, deserve a lot.'

'Love as if you've never been hurt.'
proverb

I was grateful for everything in my life. It's in our nature to always want more, to never be fully satisfied. Knowing when enough is enough requires a balance we must find within ourselves. I was beginning to feel ready to examine who I truly was – a person to be proud of, or the opposite. The source of my courage was Martin. His appearance in my life was like that epic moment in a movie that turns the tides. I felt complete, as if I could see clearly and breathe with full lungs. And everything looked, sounded and felt different, somewhat brighter, fuller, and lively.

Every challenge I'd faced left its trace on my soul and heart. Every shed tear and open wound were carefully locked in the drawers of my mind too many times to count. So many people, dear friends, acquaintances, and lovers, had appeared in my life. Some invaded, others entered through a naively open door, stealing, breaking things until the moment they finally left. Now, with all that behind me, I was a happy and grateful person, free from the grip of resentment, my heart healed and ready, not naive but wise enough to make space for the best in life. And all of this was thanks to *love*. If only more people could experience this, what a different world it would be.

The familiar dream that had haunted me for some time kept coming to me at night. Part of me had expected it to stop with Martin's wonderful eyes in my waking life now, but if anything it now felt stronger, more urgent, more lucid, and it had changed. I no longer saw the eyes waiting for me; I think I had found the answer to the question of who they belonged to. I now saw a young girl. I couldn't see her face, but I felt the pull of her existence deep within me. She wouldn't speak or move. She would simply stand there, looking at me, as though waiting, and I would stand there, looking right back at her.

I often found myself waking up from this dream with tears in my eyes, unsure of how to make sense of it.

***'It's not as difficult to die for a friend,
but to find a friend who deserves to die for …'***
proverb

'Well, tell me, how's the new job,' Lucy asked. She was excited for me.

We sat in a fine restaurant, finally having our long-postponed girls' night. Though we stayed in touch daily, we didn't have the time to meet as often. It felt odd to be in such a sophisticated place – no park benches or fast food as was our tradition when we used to work together. It seemed everything around us had changed, just as we had.

Lucy looked at me impatiently, her chin resting on her hand.

'Well'—I took a breath—'it's definitely different from my last one.'

We both laughed at the obvious fact.

'You look different,' she said, 'in the best way, of course. No more jeans and T-shirts. Most importantly, you're free from the days of work-hardened hands. I'm so proud of you, and I'm glad I'm here by your side through these big changes in your life.' She got a bit emotional.

'Oh Lucy.' I reached across the table to take her hand, tears welling up. 'We're both going through big changes! Look at you – manager now, dressed stylishly. No more sneakers, I see!'

She was right, of course. With my elegant dress and heels, I didn't look anything like the girl I was two years ago when we first met. She, too, had transformed. She looked like an adult. Despite how much our lives had changed, the unshakable bond between Lucy and me was stronger than ever – as if our friendship was older than we were.

'If anyone looked at us now,' Lucy said, 'they'd think we'd literally just complimented each other until we both started crying.'

That thought had us both laughing until our sides hurt.

The waiter arrived with our orders. With martinis in hand, we continued chatting. We both had a lot to share, news and surprises. I hadn't realised how much I'd missed her. I never expected to meet a true friend when I moved here, nor to find so much else that had felt out of reach back home. That's why the world is so vast – to give us all a chance to find our best corners.

'So'—she leaned forward, and a familiar glint came into her eye—'what's new with you and Martin?' She literally waggled her eyebrows at me, and I felt myself blush.

'Nothing new. We're just … in love,' I said with a shrug, trying to downplay it, but she wasn't having it.

'Oh, come on, Patty.'

'Well,' I sighed, knowing she wouldn't stop until I indulged her, 'we've talked a bit about maybe upgrading to a small house. We're both doing well in our jobs, and it seems like a reasonable next step.'

Her jaw dropped and her eyes widened.

'Imagine,' I continued, happy to see her reaction, 'you could come over for barbecues in the garden or sunbathe with cocktails!'

The picture I was painting had me swooning, but Lucy stayed silent, studying me.

'Don't you like the idea?'

'Oh, I like it,' she said, 'but let's talk about that idea later. I think there's something else in the air.'

'I'm not following …'

'Where are you hiding it?' she grinned.

'Hiding what?' I couldn't hold back my laugh – I couldn't follow her line of logic.

'The ring! Don't play with me, Patty. I wasn't born yesterday. This all has proposal vibes!' She leaned back, looking entirely pleased with herself, like she'd just cracked some code.

I felt heat rising in my cheeks. Apparently, *I was born yesterday* because the thought hadn't even crossed my mind. And no, there was no ring secretly weighing on my hand.

'It's not what you think, Lucy. It's just two people making a logical, practical decision. That's it,' I said, trying to stay grounded.

'Oh, please! There's always a plan,' she insisted. 'And you're just blissfully unaware because it's meant to be a surprise. I mean – don't women usually sense these things?'

I shook my head, but her words planted seeds somewhere deep inside me, creating a tiny, growing sense of hope. Though I knew how deeply we loved each other, I was still resistant to letting myself think about marriage, too fearful that Martin hadn't imagined our future in the same way.

'We've never discussed it,' I admitted, playing with the napkin in front of me. 'We've talked about almost everything else, but never *that*. I don't know if it's because he's not ready or if it just … hasn't come up.'

'Do you want it?'

I looked down, nodding. When I looked back up, my eyes were misty, not from sadness but pure joy at the thought of standing beside him, in white, united as we already were in spirit. 'I can't imagine my life without him.'

'*Thought: a conversation of the soul with yourself.*'
Plato

In rare moments, I'd let my mind wander, envisioning that perfect wedding day and wondering how we'd celebrate. There was no proposal yet, and it felt too soon to let my mind get carried away, but Lucy had opened Pandora's box with her teasing, and now the thoughts lingered. I knew Martin's family was deeply religious, so I sometimes questioned whether I'd need to carry out a traditional celebration for the big day. So much felt uncertain, but I knew one thing for sure: I had long ago broken the thread connecting me to religion …

'All religions are founded on the fear of the many and the cleverness of the few.'
Stendhal

* * *

'If God did not exist, it would be necessary to invent him'
Voltaire

* * *

'Every great religion begins with light. But only the hearts bring light. Paper cannot.'
Richard Bach

'… Come on, kids, faster! We're late for the service,' my mother urged us as we hurried down the street towards the church. Maggie and I held her hands, struggling to keep up. It was Easter, one of the few times a year we'd attend church together. My parents were always too busy otherwise, and I couldn't say I minded – it was often dull, and despite my attempts to sit quietly, I'd inevitably start looking around, curious about everything.

'Why isn't daddy coming?' Maggie asked.

I already knew the answer. It was one of the perks of being the older sister.

'Because your father isn't exactly a believer,' my mother said, sighing as she paid for candles at the entrance. I'd never heard them talk about it, but I knew Dad disliked church, and Mom had long since stopped trying to convince him otherwise. 'You can't force belief on someone,' she continued. 'If he doesn't want to come, he has every right to stay home.'

'But … is daddy a Christian?' my younger sister persisted.

'Of course he's a Christian, dear,' my mother whispered, handing us each a candle. 'He just doesn't believe as strongly as some.'

I wondered why my dad could choose not to come but I couldn't. No one ever asked me if I wanted to go; it was simply treated as a given, with no room for objection. I was only eleven, but I remember challenging my mother about it one day. She'd been both surprised and slightly lost for words, ending our conversation with, '*You have a sharp mind, sweetheart – maybe you'll make a fine lawyer someday.*' She hadn't really answered my questions, and I had no interest in being a lawyer.

A few days later, I found my mother visibly upset, and that scared me. I'd never seen her look weak; she'd always been my steady foundation. Dad was by her side, rubbing her shoulders silently, wearing that helpless expression I knew well, the one that said he wanted to help but wasn't sure how.

'Mummy?' I approached her and slipped my hand into hers. She was holding a napkin, using it to dab her wet face.

'Oh, Patty …' I could see her lower lip trembling, and then something in her expression changed. It became firm, decisive, even sharp. 'From now on, we're not going to church anymore.'

Her voice didn't sound angry, but I was still frightened. What had upset her so much that it made her change her mind about something that she had fervently defended to that day?

'Why?' It was all I managed to ask.

I noticed the quick, tense look that passed between my parents.

'I don't think she's grown enough,' my father frowned, apparently against explaining the reason.

'I think that hiding the truth'—she looked at him for a brief moment, and his eyes showed that he knew exactly what she was going to say—'is the worst thing to do—'

'Enough!' my father interrupted. 'Patty, go to your room and help Maggie with her homework.'

My mother was dabbing at her face again, and though I was still tugged by curiosity as to why we wouldn't be going to church anymore, I felt a strong urge not to know the answer.

'People were created to be loved. Things were created to be used. The reason why the world is in chaos, is because things are being loved and people are being used.'
Jonathan Moldu

* * *

'Woe betide to the one that forsakes the eternal things for the transits that pass away like the clouds. His heart will never experience peace, and his mind will fly like a boat in a storm.'
'Pharaoh' by Boleslaw Prus

By now, my job wasn't 'new' anymore. I was comfortable and confident, enough that I'd stopped worrying about my performance. It was a small private company run by a driven woman, Lindsay, whose ambition was both impressive and intimidating. I'd felt eager to prove myself at first, pouring all my energy into the workplace, but as the initial excitement faded, I began noticing things that made me question what was truly 'right' in life.

It was Lindsay's 40th birthday. She had a petite figure, well-kept, almost too thin; she was dressed in high-end designer clothes that made you dream of wearing them yourself. She had two luxury cars, a two-story mansion, and enough gold jewellery on her hands to fund a few months of my salary. Every morning, this one being no exception, she'd arrive with her hair perfectly styled, no doubt by a salon. She was someone many would envy. I, however, was an exception; I could see beyond the beautiful picture, and what I saw I didn't like.

'How long should I wait?' Lindsay snapped as she stepped out of her office. Her expression was a stark contrast to what Daisy, a work friend of mine, and I had hoped for the day, given the occasion.

'Sorry for the delay, but we ... we prepared a little surprise,' Daisy, her secretary and most trusted person, said as she held out the cake we'd picked up from the pastry shop.

I stood by, excited to see her reaction. Lindsay sighed, as though forcing herself to suppress her annoyance. She stepped out just far enough to see the cake before her expression flattened again.

'You didn't have to,' she said. 'Just put it in the fridge. Help yourselves at lunch. Daisy, I need you focused! And I'll stay late today so prepare yourself for some extra hours.'

With that, she turned and walked back into her office. I tried to keep my shock hidden, but Daisy, unfazed, shrugged as she packed the cake away.

'This is just how she is,' Daisy said quietly when she saw my face. 'I've worked for her for years – nothing surprises me anymore.'

'Then why even bother with the cake?' I asked.

Daisy looked at me for a moment. She frowned and gave a shrug. 'She has no one else. If I don't do it, who would?' With that, she headed off to the kitchen.

I returned to my work, my mind lost in thought. I'd already known Lindsay was alone – no partner, children, not even a pet. All the wealth in the world and only herself to share it with, and barely even that since she spent most of her time at work. The real question was why she'd allowed herself to end up here, and what mattered most: the power and comfort that money could provide or the warmth and love of family. I didn't have to think long for my answer, but I knew there were many people who might choose differently – Lindsay, for example.

As my workday ended, I waved goodbye to Daisy, who was staying late and didn't seem particularly disappointed with the idea as the extra hours paid double. Maybe that was why Lindsay kept her close; perhaps, in the end, they weren't so different.

I got out of the building and had just reached for my phone to call Martin when I heard a familiar voice:

'It's dangerous to walk with your eyes on your phone. You could run into someone.'

I looked up, startled, to see Martin leaning casually against a street pole, just as he had the first time we met. But everything was different now. He was mine.

'One who doesn't adore the shortcomings of the one they love cannot claim to really be in love.'
Pedro Calderon

* * *

'If you judge people, you will not have time to love them.'
Mother Teresa

'... Patty, honey ... I'm sorry to bother you like this, but I really need someone to talk to ...' Lucy's voice said through the phone, thick with tears.

'I saw you'd called three times, so I figured it must be important. And you can never bother me – don't say that,' I gently scolded her. 'I asked for an early lunch break so I could call you right back. Now, tell me what's going on ...'

Lucy sighed – a sound so heavy it practically radiated her sadness. My worry grew, but I stayed silent, letting her start when she was ready.

'It's about Ben. I just ... don't even know how to put it into words. It feels like everything's happening at once, and I have no idea what to do ...'

Ben had been her boyfriend for a year, a relationship that started with the same intensity that everything in Lucy's life seemed to have. I'd liked him from the beginning; he was perfect for her, like Martin was for me. But love was powerful, and it sometimes scared people when they sensed its intensity.

'All right, sweetie, take a deep breath and start from the beginning,' I said, hoping to calm her and make sense of what she was saying.

'I think things between us aren't going well,' she finally said. 'There's just so much about him that irritates me now, and every day, something new comes up. I've told him so many times not to do certain things, but he just doesn't listen! Like smoking – it's such a bad habit! I keep telling him to quit, but he keeps doing it. I don't know ... I'm just so frustrated!' She was speaking so quickly I could barely keep up. Despite myself, I laughed, interrupting her before she spiralled further.

'Okay, listen to me,' I said. 'I'll tell you the secret to a happy relationship.'

'Patty, I'm serious. I'm really upset!' she insisted. I could tell she was getting irritated with me.

'I know, honey. I can hear it in your voice. But stop for just a second and listen. Maybe what I have to say will help, but the choice is yours, of course.' A silence followed, which I took as a hesitant agreement, though I could practically see her pouting on the other end of the line. 'You used to smoke yourself not so long ago.'

'But I quit, remember? I realised how nasty it was.'

'Yes, and that was your personal choice. No one forced you.' I emphasised my point, hoping she'd understand. When she sighed, I took it as my cue to keep going.

'Lucy, a relationship is like a fragile crystal, a place for love, respect, and shared energy. Everyone seems to think that finding love is the hard part, but that's just the beginning. Once you've found your person, the challenge is to preserve that love while protecting yourselves too.'

'What do you mean by "protecting yourselves"?' Lucy asked, sceptical.

'It means you have to learn self-control because too much or too little of yourself can damage that crystal. Being in a relationship doesn't mean you make the other person submit to you. Love sometimes triggers this odd sense of ownership, but to love is to respect your partner's life – including all the habits that existed long before you came along. It's selfish to expect them to change everything at your command, to make themselves a blank slate for you to "improve". Love means giving each other space to breathe and be free. It's far better to let him choose to be with you because he feels free to do so, not because he feels bound to. Love requires trust, and you can't let it twist into jealousy, doubt, or obsession.'

'To be made of tears and sighs, of flame and loyalty, until you're nothing but ashes,' Lucy cut in.

'Shakespeare!' I laughed. 'Of course, great minds like his are always right, which is why these words live on. But let's be honest – that's a bit too dramatic. My view of love is more optimistic than ending up as a pile of ashes.'

Our sudden laughter lifted the weight of the conversation. Lucy sighed again, but this time she sounded calmer.

'Patty, I don't know about Shakespeare, but your advice always helps me. Who knows, maybe one day people will repeat your words like they do his?'

'Ha! Lucy, please!' I couldn't stop laughing. 'I'm just happy if my words help you out now and then. I'm nowhere near Shakespeare.'

'I love you, Patty. I don't know what I'd do without you ...'

*'It is stupid to make plans for a lifetime,
when you are not the master of tomorrow.'*
Seneca

As I finished my makeup, I felt a sneeze coming on. I tried to hold it in without luck. When I opened my eyes, I was horrified to see that my mascara had smudged under my eyes and across my eyelids.

'Great!' I muttered, frowning at my reflection. My mood was sinking fast. I barely had time to fix the slip before I had to fly out the door, so I decided to do my lipstick and hair on the underground on my way to work.

I was one of the last to get on the train, which was packed as usual. Finding a seat was out of the question, so I tried to apply my lipstick standing up. Just as I steadied myself, the girl next to me stumbled while rummaging through her bag – my lipstick ended up across my chin.

'I'm so sorry,' she apologised, turning to hold tight before causing another incident.

I sighed. Could my day be any worse? I grabbed a tissue to clean my face just as my stop was announced. I rushed out, wiping blindly at my chin and hoping I didn't look too ridiculous by the time I reached the office.

Arriving at the building, I was surprised to find a crowd gathered outside, but I didn't have time to linger. I rushed in and nearly collided with Daisy.

'Why didn't you answer your phone?' she snapped, not even saying hello. She looked genuinely stressed, biting her lip and running a hand through her hair.

'I'm sorry—'

'Why is your chin all red?'

'I—uh, it's just lipstick,' I mumbled. But as I watched her, I realised something serious was going on. 'I'll stay late if I need to catch up,' I offered, thinking I made Lindsay upset with my late arrival.

'What are you talking about?' she asked. 'No one noticed you were late, Patty. There's a much bigger issue. Lindsay ... I found her unconscious this morning.'

I gasped, clapping my hands over my mouth.

'I don't know how long she was like that. I called an ambulance, and they took her right away. I was trying to reach you to let you know that you didn't need to come in today.'

'Did the doctors say anything?' I barely got the words out.

'No, but I'm going to the hospital to wait for news. We'll have to keep the office closed until she's back ...'

'Closed?' I repeated, barely able to process it. 'For how long?'

'I don't know, Patty. Let's just hope she's all right ...' Daisy's eyes welled up, and I could see how much Lindsay meant to her. I hugged her tightly.

'She'll be fine,' I said, trying to comfort her. 'She's just overworked – that's all. But if you need anything, even just some company, I'm here.'

'Thanks.' Daisy managed a small smile. 'For now, just go home. I'll keep you posted.'

As she walked out, I stood there in shock. I was supposed to go home, but I felt unable to move, my mind reeling with questions. And now what? Would I be without work indefinitely? My God, how selfish was I to worry about work when Lindsay's life was at stake?

On the train back, I stared out the window, watching the city blur by without really seeing anything. Finally home, I tossed my keys onto the table, kicked off my shoes, and sank into the couch, trying to make sense of everything that had just happened.

It was terrible – no one deserved to end up that way. Poor Lindsay was completely alone and consumed by work, with no one to look out for her in a moment like this. I hoped she appreciated Daisy's loyalty. The whole thing felt rather tragic. But I had to think about myself as well – what would I do? Martin and I talked about leaving our cramped apartment for a house, about travelling the world together. How could I do any of that if I lost my job? How had everything turned upside down overnight? I checked my phone for messages or missed calls, but there was nothing. Disappointed, I put it down and closed my eyes. If Daisy called, I'd hear it. for now, I just needed a moment ...

> **'The human race has improved almost everything, but the human race.'**
> Stevenson

Fortunately, Lindsay wouldn't go down that easily – she had too much work to do to be bothered by something like death. Two weeks passed since the incident, and life had already returned to its usual pace, more or less. Lindsay was up and working within three days. Rather, she was in bed with a laptop. She'd been warned by her doctor to take it easy – work stress, smoking, caffeine overload, and practically no food had put her there – but no one could tell Lindsay what to do, and if someone didn't know that, they'd learn it very quickly. I was initially overjoyed to hear she was safe, but back in the office, I realised my feelings were less joy and more relief.

The anxiety that gripped me over losing my job had obviously lasted only a few days, during which Martin did everything he could to reassure me that, no matter what, we'd be fine as long as we had each other, but though his words were a comfort, I didn't fully relax until I received a message from Daisy confirming Lindsay was back.

Work resumed as though nothing had happened. After a few days of bed work, Lindsay was walking in and out of her office, giving orders in her standard reactive fashion, keeping everyone on edge. It was hard to sympathise with her even after what she'd gone through. Still, I couldn't help but wonder – if it had been me, would I have come out unaffected? Wouldn't I, after such a close call, begin to see life differently? Grateful to still be here, wouldn't I see life as something precious, something to appreciate rather than take for granted? Or maybe that was just me, romanticising things again.

'Do not expect much from the fire that burns everything.
Do not expect much of the wealth where everything is lost.
Do not expect much from the day when the Sun sets.
Do not regret what you remember. Do not look at the good that seduces – it is not for you. Remember ... you are not sent to the world to resolve all the controversies, but you are sent to live. If you learn this, you will get a lot, and if you do not learn it, you still have to learn ...'
proverb

At 16:30, I grabbed my bag, wished Daisy a nice evening, and left the office. The fresh air outside made me feel better, easing the dull pulse in my head. It was Friday – the end of the workweek – and while I'd normally rush home, I knew Martin wouldn't be there yet. So, I made a split-second decision to do something different, something I rarely found time for with my hectic routine.

The day was crisp and bright, the cold air biting just a little, but I didn't mind. Wrapping my scarf more tightly around me, I crossed the street to a small park I'd only glimpsed in passing when Martin picked me up from work. *Have I really become so immersed in city life that even a few minutes in a nearby park feels like an adventure?* I wondered.

My life had changed completely since coming to London, and while I didn't regret it, I sometimes missed the slower pace. I sat on the first empty bench I found, which faced a small pond. Wrapping my arms around myself, against the chill, I smiled at a mother duck floating by, trailed by her ducklings. They glided past another duck who was diving for food. Nature – how effortlessly it could bring peace and joy.

'Ah, what a day!' a voice said, startling me; I hadn't realised someone else was on the bench – in fact, I could have sworn I was the only one seated there. An elderly woman sat at the other end, smiling in my direction.

'Yes … a beautiful day,' I replied with a polite smile, glancing back at the pond.

She rummaged in her bag and pulled out a packet of biscuits, offering one to me with a warm, inviting smile.

'Oh, no thank you,' I declined politely, but she simply shrugged and broke one in half, keeping one piece for herself while holding the other outstretched, palm up. I wondered why for a moment, but then a pigeon landed on her hand and began to nibble at it.

'We must share in this life, my dear,' she said, looking at me. She winked, sending my mind straight to Lucy. There was a beauty in her simple gesture. Watching her, I found myself thinking how rare it was these days to meet someone who radiated kindness as she did, someone who still seemed genuinely grateful for each day.

'You are right,' I nodded, 'it's a shame many people are afraid to make such small gestures these days.'

She turned to me with a nod of agreement, placing half a biscuit in my hand. As another pigeon flew over and landed on me, a small laugh bubbled up and out my mouth, but I quickly calmed myself down, not wanting to startle it. Such a simple thing, but it made me feel unexpectedly light and happy.

'The worst part,' she said, her gaze soft on the bird, 'is thinking we give away everything without a reward.'

I stayed there for another half hour, chatting about everything and nothing with the nice stranger. When I finally said goodbye and made my way home, I felt my smile stuck on my face, not fading for anything.

'I'm waiting for you, because I love miracles.'
P.K. Yavorov

When I woke up in the morning, I had vague dream memories – they were fading fast: I was already married to someone who I knew to be Martin, only it didn't quite look like him. I had children too, but their faces weren't familiar to me.

'Love, I'm heading out. Have a great day,' Martin said, kissing me gently. His touch pulled me from my thoughts.

'You too. I'd better hurry, or I'll be late again,' I replied, a bit tense.

'Everything alright?' he asked. I felt his eyes were scrutinising me a bit too closely.

'Yes, yes, totally,' I assured him, overreacting slightly. 'I just had a strange dream, that's all.'

'Tell me about it after work?' His expression shifted slightly, almost imperceptibly, but I'd come to know every subtle line and wrinkle on his face. I could sense a hint of discomfort there, though he tried to mask it. 'And I'd like us to have dinner together tonight.'

'We always have dinner together,' I said, confused. He cleared his throat and hurried to the door as though he suddenly remembered he might be late.

'I mean at a restaurant. Get ready, and let's meet at our favourite spot at eight. Bye.' Before I could respond, he was out the door, leaving me to wonder what could be behind such a spontaneous plan. It was just a dinner, but my instinct told me there was more to it. I'd always been a bit of a pessimist – maybe overly so – but I couldn't shake the feeling that something was coming.

The workday blurred by – I felt like I was barely present. My mind kept replaying the strange morning. A nagging feeling was tugging at me, but my intuition, however sharp, wasn't always spot on. I'd learned over the years to trust my inner voice and pay attention to signs, but that didn't mean they were always clear or that I interpreted them correctly. Even though my senses often guided me well, they'd also misled me when tangled with misplaced wishes and stubbornness. Still, I kept running over theories about what Martin might have on his mind and why he'd chosen our favourite restaurant. It was a very fancy place, and we usually went there on special occasions, so his invitation sparked more curiosity than excitement.

As I left the office, my phone rang. I fumbled for it, finally finding it buried in my purse. It was Lucy.

'Hello?' I answered.

'Hey, sweetie, how are you?' She sounded cheerful.

'Fine. Just leaving work.'

'What's wrong? You don't sound good.'

'No, everything is fine,' I insisted, not wanting to dig into the odd details of my day.

She sighed. 'Alright, let's try that again. What's really going on? You don't sound good at *all*.'

Lucy knew me so well, and while I loved her, sometimes I preferred to keep my thoughts to myself.

'I just didn't sleep well,' I admitted. 'And then this morning, it seemed like Martin was acting ... I don't know, kind of strange. Almost like he was in a rush to escape the apartment while inviting me to dinner.' Saying it out loud didn't make me feel any better.

'Maybe you're overthinking it. Men can be so oblivious sometimes,' she teased, then added, 'Have you decided what to wear?'

And just like that, I was reminded of how often I tended to make something out of nothing. Either I was losing my mind, or I simply needed a new hobby. But Lucy's reaction wasn't at all in her style; usually she'd dive into a detailed analysis of Martin's behaviour, dissecting every shade instead of glossing over it.

'I haven't thought about it yet,' I admitted as I passed my oyster travel card through the machine. 'Look, Lucy, I need to catch the train. How about I call you later this week?'

'No problem. Just hang on – one last thing. I picture you in that red off-the-shoulder dress. You'd look amazing!'

'You mean Martin's favourite? It's too formal for a casual dinner.'

'Why settle for "a casual dinner"? Has the spark already faded?' I could actually hear the smile on her face. 'Shake things up a bit!'

I didn't know why she was insisting so strongly, but she made a fair point.

'Alright, I'll think about it, but I really have to go.' I said goodbye and slipped into the train, still puzzled over why the simplest thing felt so strange today.

Arriving home, I found the apartment empty. It was still early, but I knew Martin would be back soon, so I decided to take a quick shower. As the warm water poured over me, I felt the day's tension melt away. By the time I stepped out, I was finally feeling a bit more like myself. I wrapped a towel around me and was about to get dressed when I noticed a small piece of paper on my side of the bed:

Love, our reservation is for 20:00.
Dress code is elegant.
Meet you there.
Martin

So he wasn't coming home first. But how did the note get there? I looked at my wardrobe and, as if on cue, the red dress Lucy had suggested seemed to glow from among the other clothes. Her advice suddenly felt all too fitting.

I put on the dress, adjusting it until it hugged every curve perfectly. It was a classic style, knee-length with one strap and the other side off the shoulder. I tied my hair back and put on long earrings that framed my neck elegantly. A touch of dark eye makeup added the right amount of mystery, and as I glanced in the mirror, a nervous smile broke through. Tonight, I actually felt ... beautiful.

The restaurant was close by, but I called a taxi. Martin had always urged me to drive more, but my sluggish 2-km-per-hour pace didn't inspire anyone's confidence. London's left-side driving only added to my hesitance. Tonight, my safe and only alternative was a taxi.

Stepping out of the car, I entered the familiar restaurant. A hostess greeted me warmly. 'Good evening, madam. I believe there's a reservation for you.'

'Yes, at eight,' I replied. I was smiling, but I felt my nerves were obvious.

'The gentleman is waiting for you. This way, please.'

Following her, we passed tables filled with couples and families. She led me to a secluded door, which I hadn't noticed before. Inside, a smaller, more intimate room appeared, its dim light casting a cosy, almost magical, glow.

The hostess helped me with my coat as I finally saw him. He stood as I approached, his eyes lighting up, though his brow glistened with a faint trace of nervous sweat. He gave me a quick kiss on the lips, then pulled out my chair, all while managing to look so composed.

'Are we celebrating something?' I asked, scanning my memory for a forgotten date. He raised his glass and looked at me intently.

'I hope so,' he replied softly, lifting his glass. 'Cheers.'

His words sent me back to the evening he'd invited me to move in with him. It had been in much humbler surroundings, my little single room, but I remembered the same thrill of expectation as he held a glass of wine. He looked at me now with that same nervous intensity, and I felt my heart beat faster.

'You look beautiful,' he said, his voice a little unsteady, and for once, I couldn't argue. His eyes were fixed on me, like an anchor to the shore, full of adoration and something else I hadn't figured out yet.

'And you look different …' I began, struggling to find the right words.

He cleared his throat and took another sip. I followed his lead, letting the sparkling alcohol pour into my mouth like water. It didn't help much – my head was already swimming – but at least it steadied my trembling hands.

'I've been thinking about this a lot lately … about how to say it,' he continued, his voice suddenly more serious.

His words hit me like a sharp blade to the stomach, making me instinctively shrink back. I didn't want to drink, or eat, or even breathe – I just wanted to hear the rest of what he had to say.

'I couldn't come to a decision.' He lifted his head, meeting my gaze again. 'You know I'm not as emotional as you are, but what I need to say requires a bit more expression – pardon me if it doesn't feel as natural.'

I listened, but the only sound I could hear was the ticking of an invisible clock counting down the seconds to what I feared would be bad news. I didn't want to give in to these dark thoughts, but they continued to creep in, relentless and unavoidable. Could it be happening? A separation? Lost love? No, I would collapse here, now and forever. If he left, it wouldn't just be the end of our relationship – it would be the end of everything, my future, my dreams, the very spark that kept my soul alive.

'My wish,' he said slowly, 'isn't based on the years we've spent together, because they're only two. It's not about societal expectations either. My wish isn't based on tradition or natural continuity. I want you to know that meeting you, having you in my life ... it fills a gap I didn't even know existed.'

I blinked, utterly confused. What was he talking about?

'I wanted this day to be special, to make a good memory of it. But maybe I'm not original enough to make it as perfect as you imagined,' he continued, his eyes holding mine. 'All I know is that we both feel the same way. If you'll accept me as I am, then I ask you ... will you marry me?

His hand reached across the table, palm open, and I saw the small box resting there. Inside was a delicate gold ring, its large square stone gleaming in the dim light of the room. A few seconds passed before my eyes filled with tears, which shortly after broke free, running down my cheeks.

'Patty ...' Martin's voice cracked.

I covered my face with my hands, trying to hide my tears. I heard the chair scrape as he stood up, and a moment later, I felt him beside me, kneeling down, his hands gentle as he caressed me. 'I didn't want to upset you,' he whispered, 'only to make you happy. But if your happiness doesn't depend on me ...'

I stopped crying immediately, lowering my hands from my face to look at him in disbelief with my swollen red eyes.

'Don't you understand?' I asked with a breaking voice. 'For me, the word *happiness* doesn't exist if you aren't here! I'm not crying out of sadness. I can't believe my luck ... to have everything I've ever wanted. I'm crying because this moment is a dream come true, and it feels like a miracle.'

Martin looked at me, his eyes now glistening with tears, almost matching mine. Without a word, he reached out, his hand slipping gently around the back of my neck, and pulled me in for a kiss, his lips burning with love.

'I love you!' he whispered

'I love you ...' I echoed with a full heart.

Later, I realised there was no way I could surprise Lucy with the news of the engagement, as she obviously knew about it before I did. That explained the strange conversation we'd had earlier and the text I received later that night:

Is the ring the right fit?
Lucy

CHAPTER II

LOVE

*'According to Greek mythology, humans were originally
created with four arms, four legs and a head with two faces.
Fearing their power, Zeus split them into two separate parts, condemning them to spend their lives looking for their other half ...'*
Plato, The Symposium

* * *

*'When a person meets his half that is his very own, whatever
his orientation, whether it's a young man or not, then
something wonderful happens: the two are struck
from their senses by love, by a sense of belonging to one
another and by desire, and they do not want to be
separated from each other even for a moment ...'*
Aristophanes, The Symposium

Another day had passed, much like the one before it, yet with something different. I opened the front door as I arrived home, and a natural smile spread across my face. Martin was waiting for me. Nothing unusual about that, but still, day after day, my heart raced wildly with excitement. I threw myself in his arms like a child seeking comfort from their mother and kissed him with the passion of lovers reunited after a long separation. Would this obsessive longing ever wane? I hoped not. It was what kept me alive – a pure, inexplicable happiness that transcended anything I had ever known.

'Hey,' he laughed, breathless from my fervent embrace. 'How are you, love?' he asked and gently kissed my forehead.

The effect he had on me was astonishing. The world around us faded, leaving only him. Looking into his fiery brown eyes, I sighed and replied, 'Well, usually tired, but it doesn't matter anymore.' My eyes narrowed playfully. 'I think today is the perfect day for that bath we talked about.'

'What bath …?'

If I hadn't known him so well, I might have believed him. But Martin was neither a convincing actor nor a particularly skilled liar. It was my boundless naivety that made me hesitate. Sometimes I wondered why I didn't work harder to overcome it – being naive wasn't exactly a desirable trait, especially in a world populated by the most dangerous species of all: people.

'I don't recall any such thing,' Martin continued. 'That's why I didn't prepare the bathtub.' He broke into a smile, dropping the act.

I sank into the bath and the hot water instantly soothed my stiff muscles. The thick white foam covering the surface had a nice aroma, which I inhaled deeply with eyes closed.

If only I could indulge in this luxury every day – followed by a massage and a long, uninterrupted sleep – that would be the perfect routine. But such indulgence wasn't my fate, at least not in this life. Still, I had something that compensated for it all.

Lying against his chest, I needed nothing more in this magical moment. Martin held my hands in his, kissing them tenderly, as we sat together in tranquil silence. Our relationship was beyond anything I'd ever experienced. Still, I sometimes wondered: was it yet more than what I realised? The profound connection we shared felt like proof that he was the other half of my soul, but ... there was something else.

That night, Martin fell asleep before me. I closed my eyes and the fatigue soon took over. My body relaxed completely, in a state between sleep and wakefulness.

Then something happened.

I tried to move my hand, but the command didn't reach my muscles. Paralysed and trapped, I felt a surge of panic. I wanted to wake Martin, but even my lips refused to move. Then a strange sensation stole my attention – movement. It wasn't frightening, but it was undeniably strange.

Images began to flicker behind my closed eyes, like a film reel unspooling. They were memories – mine. Moments from yesterday, the day before, last year, and the years before that. They shifted and flowed rapidly, a collage of joy and sorrow from my life.

The pace increased until the images blurred, replaced by unfamiliar scenes. They weren't my memories anymore. The shapes dissolved into a chaotic whirlwind, and the panic overtook me. What was I seeing? None of it made sense. Desperate, I tried to scream for help, but the thought struck me: *Whom would I scream for?* I realised I no longer knew who I was.

The images slowed, and I could see them more clearly now. Narrow, winding streets teemed with vibrant market stalls. People bustled about with their colourful garments, bright against the stone architecture. The living hum of voices filled the air in a language I couldn't place. But then, inexplicably, I understood a fruit seller speaking with a woman, bargaining the price.

The scene shifted again.

Inside a wealthy house, a curvy, young woman yelled. 'Why is the servant not here yet?'

Her irritated expression made it clear she was waiting for something – and losing patience. Opposite her sat another woman, lean and sharp-featured, whose smirk suggested she was enjoying her friend's frustration. It could easily be said that both women weren't the town's beauties, but they were wealthy, and like most cases in life – one justified the other.

'I ordered the bath to be ready before I finished my dessert, and I'm still waiting!' the same woman snapped again; her face flushed with anger, and her small eyes stared wildly, ready to pop out of their sockets.

'Oh, Flavia, darling! I think your appetite has outpaced events once again,' her friend laughed loudly, in amusement.

'Oh, you are unbearable, Cecilia ...'

The scene shifted once more.

A short, balding man in a white robe burst through the doors of what appeared to be an office. There were guards at the entrance and servants in the corners of the spacious room. Behind a large desk with unfolded pieces of parchment, sat a man with piercing blue eyes and dark blond hair. He looked almost handsome, but his facial features were strict and radiated authority. He was clearly of a high rank.

'Prefect,' the short man greeted, bowing his head with a smile that seemed anything but genuine. 'I must once again raise the urgent matter of the riots in the city's outskirts. The situation is out of control and swift action is required!'

He was interrupted by the Prefect, whose sudden irritation was clear.

'Must I remind you, Maurizio, that I decide what is required?' His tone softened as he continued, 'We'll address it at the council. Calm yourself. You see only military solutions to every problem, but peace must prevail. These are not times for unnecessary bloodshed.'

'As you command, Prefect …' Maurizio didn't seem to agree, but he slowly retreated with an irritated expression, partially concealed by a humble smile.

I didn't like this man.

Scene after scene shifted, like in a dream where I was merely a spectator, and the characters were strangers. I thought my imagination must have taken a dangerous turn, yet the intrusive feeling that everything was somehow real refused to leave me.

Suddenly the fog lifted. There were no more unfolding storylines, no unfamiliar faces – just one face staring back at me. A reflection in a mirror. It was me. I stood there in the flesh, seated before a richly decorated mirror. The dressing table in front of me was covered with delicate glass bottles of perfume, jewellery boxes, and other luxurious items. I examined myself with curiosity, almost uncertainty, as though seeing my own reflection for the first time. My long chestnut hair was pleasantly shaped in gentle curls. My almond-shaped eyes were beautifully highlighted with makeup. Draped around me was an ivory silk robe, edged with embroidery.

The sound of a door opening drew me out of my own reflection and I jumped in fright.

'My dear, good morning,' came a warm voice. It was my mother, Agostina.

The scattered pieces of information about my surroundings came together – this was my room, my home. A sense of comfort and security replaced my earlier confusion, but my eyes continued to see things as new and foreign.

'What is it?' she asked. Her keen perception missed nothing.

'Good morning, mother. I'm just waking up – give me a moment.' I smiled, but it didn't seem to convince her.

'I'll order for your breakfast to be set on the terrace. Perhaps the fresh air will help,' she offered. She seemed to hold her breath for a moment, a word stuck on her tongue. 'Was it another one of *those* dreams?'

Her question was not unexpected. Even I sometimes worried about the strange adventures my dreaming mind tended to set out on. I almost never understood the meaning of them, but my mother was always beside me to listen patiently and direct me.

'Nothing to worry about, mother,' I assured her more confidently as I made myself believe it too.

That seemed to satisfy her, at least for the moment, and she went on cheerfully. To my regret, the subject of the conversation took a less pleasant turn.

'You haven't forgotten that Cornelius Scepion will visit today?' Her reminder wasn't necessary, but she wanted me to know how important this visit was. 'I'll be back shortly to help you prepare,' she added with a calm yet purposeful voice.

The smile on her face was one I didn't want to spoil, but it was inevitable that I would.

'Mother, you know my opinion. I can give you my answer before the visit even begins.' I allowed my irritation to prevail in my voice, but I instantly regretted my outburst. I didn't intend for my emotions to hurt her, and I glanced at her quickly. Her expression remained the same, as though she hadn't heard me – or perhaps she simply chose not to acknowledge it.

'I'll be right back,' she said, and vanished through the door.

I knew she was tired of our endless debates on the matter, and I could sense her frustration with my stubbornness, but I also knew she wouldn't surrender. That was the hidden message behind her powerful tone – my choices were not mine to make.

I turned back to the mirror, meeting my reflection again. The visit I expected was in my honour, but I felt no joy, no anticipation. And the reason? My beauty. Throughout the city, they said I was without compare. Attention like this would have surely delighted any other girl, but not me. I was different, and I knew it. I didn't fit into the society around me, and the thought that I might never belong pursued me relentlessly. Instead, I dreamed of escape – of a life far away where I could live freely. At that moment, I felt like a withering flower among weeds, fighting for air. I couldn't survive much longer like this. Yet, the attention never waned. Suitors came from the city and even from distant places to ask for my hand while women resented me for the very thing I wished I could escape. I didn't want their admiration or envy. I wanted freedom and love – not the shallow kind of love that masked greed and base desires. I wanted something beautiful, something true – a love that bound two souls together for eternity.

In the harsh reality of life, there was no room for my dreams – yet I nourished them, thanks to my mother. I often wondered why she, who had taught me about freedom and love, now insisted that I choose a husband from among the suitors. My mother had always said we should never enslave our souls, and yet here she was, asking me to make a choice based not on love but on strategy.

I grew up in a respected family. Although not part of the highest elite, we lived comfortably, distinct from the lower classes. My parents, Agostina and Emiliy, had chosen a quiet life, avoiding political alliances and conflicts. Some might have seen this as a disgrace, but I admired them for it. They taught me to live with my eyes wide open.

My mother often reminded me that *'everything in life is a balance'*. If today you are born a noble, then in the next life, you could be someone's servant. I was taught to respect people, nature, and the gods alike. I never flaunted my status, aware of the fragile line separating fortune and misfortune. Walking through the streets, I'd often see innocent faces marked by the cruel hand of hardship. Meanwhile, among the aristocracy, many clung to the belief that gold could buy a place among the gods. The Earth, it seemed, was full of 'immortal and omnipotent' souls who crushed others under the weight of their ambitions, leaving the pure-hearted to suffer in poverty and slavery.

The sound of the doors opening pulled me from my thoughts yet again. My mother entered with her usual serene smile, ready once more to tackle my stubbornness. I admired her for her unwavering patience and fearless determination. She had promised to teach me this art one day, claiming it was inevitable that I picked it up. And I knew why – I was different. Special. Just as she was. Ours was a family with a great secret, passed down from mother to daughter for generations.

Setting a bowl of fruit aside, she began styling my hair just like I liked.

'When was your last dream?' she asked casually, but her tone showed intention rather than simple curiosity. I didn't need to think – the memory was so vivid, etched into my mind.

'Three moons ago,' I replied. She wasn't asking about ordinary dreams, those forgotten by morning, but those profound visions that clung to me, whispering meanings I struggled to decipher.

'Do you want to share with me?' she asked, gently as always, offering me the choice. And as usual, I did want to share because these dreams weren't meant to be kept hidden.

'I was in a cave or a basement,' I began, 'lit by candles. A faint melody played somewhere in the distance, haunting and beautiful – I'd recognise it anywhere. A man stood before me. I can't recall his face, only his voice. it was deep and powerful, and it still echoes in my mind. He took my hand, gripping it tightly as though to emphasise the importance of his words: "I swear to you that you will know Love. You'll carry it within yourself and give it. The greatest power is Love." The rest of the dream … is a fog.'

When I finished, I noticed my mother had paused, her hands still in my hair. She stared at me through the mirror with an unreadable expression. A weight seemed to hang in the silence. 'You know the story of our family's origin,' she began, and I nodded quickly. She continued in a whisper, as though afraid the walls might hear.

'The gods were our ancestors, Patricia. Long ago, they chose to walk among humans, to guide and help them. To do so, they sacrificed their divine powers, taking on mortal forms and enduring the struggles of life. Their mission was noble – to save humanity from chaos, to lead lost souls towards the light. And though their divinity faded, a fragment of it was passed down through generations. The spark lives in us, guiding us, reminding us of our purpose. But humanity is not ready to see us for what we are. Their hearts are closed, their minds blind, their senses dulled. That is why we keep our nature a secret, passed from mother to daughter. Not even your father knows, and your future husband must never know either.'

She paused, her gaze piercing. 'But you must understand, Patricia, those who are different always draw attention, and with attention comes danger. I know you don't wish to marry those your father and I bring to you, but you need a man whose name will protect you, one that will ensure no one dares to question you. Only then will you be free to fulfil your destiny.'

Her words felt heavy, and I wanted to protest against the sacrifice she demanded of me, but I couldn't deny the truth in her reasoning.

'And what is my destiny, mother?' I finally asked, though deep down I suspected the answer.

'To help,' she replied. 'To bring light, to guide the lost, to give Love. That is your destiny – the destiny of our family. And you are already of age – you are eighteen, and if you don't marry soon, people will start to whisper and gossip.'

I sat in silence. A part of me was proud to be chosen for such a noble purpose, but another part longed for something more. My reflection in the mirror stared back at me, conflicted.

'Are you not happy?' my mother asked, almost in disbelief.

'Of course I am'—I forced another smile—'but how am I meant to fulfill my destiny of giving Love if I'm not left to find real love for myself.'

'Have faith,' she said gently. 'No poison can kill a positive thinker, and no medicine can save a negative one. Trust that everything will come in its time.'

Her words were comforting, but I thought of my parents' bond – a love so pure it had been my inspiration.

'You and father are so happy. That's what I want for myself,' I admitted.

'Do not compare your life with that of others,' she said firmly. 'There's no race between the Sun and the Moon. They rise when their time comes! Now let's prepare you. We shouldn't keep our guest waiting.'

We headed for the main hall, where everything had been prepared for our special guest, and where my father, Emiliy, was expecting us. He was a man who would sacrifice everything for us, and I understood why my mother had chosen him as her partner. He possessed a rare quality – true humanity. Though he had no knowledge of my mother's origin, their bond was built on pure love and mutual respect. I had always admired their relationship, and now, I faced the time of making my own choice. I didn't want a life of calm predictability with a man who would dutifully walk beside me. I longed for a love that transcended the ordinary, something almost unreal. My heart seemed to beat for him – the one I hadn't met yet. And every moment without him was a torment. Somewhere out in the world, he was searching for me, even if he didn't yet realise what he was seeking. I couldn't explain this to my mother, whose every effort was driven by her desire to protect me and our secret. To her, the preservation of that secret was as crucial as finding love was to me.

As we waited, my heart clenched at the thought of my mother's inevitable disappointment. I knew exactly how this visit would end, as had all the others before it.

'Cornelius Scepion,' the servant announced, his voice echoing through the hall.

All eyes turned to the doors as our guest entered. He strode with head held high, confidence supported by some military achievements and wealth. His soul, however, was laid bare to me, and I saw nothing I desired. Just another man enslaved by the false gods of gold and power – he was their devoted worshiper.

My parents greeted him warmly, and soon it was his turn to speak.

'Thank you for the kind welcome,' he began with a steady and deliberate voice. 'It's an honour to be in your home today. I humbly stand before you to express my desire to offer your daughter all that I possess – my estates and my heart. I assure you, there is no one in this town, or beyond, who can provide her with more than I can. I ask you for your blessing.'

He delivered his rehearsed speech with a respectable bow, then stood with a triumphant smile in expectation. My father, I knew, was touched; I didn't need to look to see it. My mother, though less visibly moved, seemed satisfied enough.

Before anyone could respond, I spoke:

'We are honoured by your interest and your visit, Cornelius Scepion,' I began, keeping my tone polite but firm. 'However, a nobleman of your rank wastes his time in the home of simple and humble citizens. Surely, someone more worthy should stand by your side.'

The room fell into stunned silence. My parents' faces were a mixture of shock and dismay at what could be perceived as bad manners. Cornelius's confidence was visibly shaken, but after a short pause, he responded:

'I ... thank you for the hospitality,' he said stiffly. Without another word, he turned and walked out with no trace of his proud smile.

I sighed in relief, but the tension didn't dissolve when our guest left. Now I had to face my parents.

'Well, we can add his name to the list of suitors rejected by our pretentious daughter,' my father remarked lightly, attempting to ease the tension. But my mother didn't respond. 'I want the best for you, my precious daughter. Believe me, I want it even more than you do. But let me offer you some advice – sometimes, in choosing too carefully, we risk having no choice at all. One day you'll have to say *yes*. He kissed my forehead and left with my mother following him. She wasn't looking at me.

Was my rejection of Cornelius seen as childish defiance? I felt sad. Why was it that what was good for one person often felt so wrong for another? And what if the love I longed for didn't exist? How could I dream of something I had never known?

'Another man's broken heart – how tragic,' a soft giggle interrupted my thoughts. I turned to see Lucretia, my personal servant and most trusted friend.

She'd been with me since childhood and was the sister I never had. We were the same age, but didn't share the same fate. And yet, she was lucky to be with my family; my parents had their moments of frustration with me, but our home was a rare haven of harmony and respect.

'What's wrong with you?' she asked, noticing my expression.

'I don't know.' I admitted with a sigh, covering my face with my hands. 'Everything is so complicated.'

'It's simple really,' she replied with a grin, 'either love sparks at first sight, or it doesn't. In this case, it clearly didn't.'

Her ability to oversimplify things had once again made me laugh. She had a real skill for lifting my spirits, even in the darkest moments.

'I have something that might interest you,' she added with a brightening tone, 'an invitation – from the Prefect himself. He's hosting a grand event in a few days. Apparently, he's celebrating his success in resolving the issue with the poor on the outskirts – peacefully, no less.'

'Are you saying he didn't send his army to crush them?' I asked in disbelief, half-intrigued.

'Seems times are changing – perhaps even for the better.'

'Hard to believe,' I murmured. 'Powerful men rarely act without bloodshed.'

'Maybe this one is different,' she suggested with a wink.

I couldn't deny that, at this point, I was intrigued. Attending the event could even lift my mother's spirits after today's disappointment. Surprisingly, the idea itself didn't repel me as much as I'd expected, which made me wonder. Usually, I didn't like attending any events, especially after I grew old enough to understand their true nature. They only offered overindulgent drinking and false smiles, and when the wine was gone so too were the morals. My reluctance to take part in it all didn't go unnoticed. Men saw me as shy and innocent while women thought me pretentious. My mother was right – drawing too much attention could be dangerous, and my *odd* behaviour only brought more of it. Something had to change, and soon.

The day of the event arrived. I woke up from another strange dream. Were these dreams mere illusions, or glimpses into another reality? Often, I would think it was the second. This time, as always, a pair of burning eyes haunted me, fog mysteriously concealing the face I wanted to see … my name was whispered in the sweetest, most familiar voice …

The journey to the mansion was short, and soon we stood in front of the massive gates. The garden with its ancient trees and ornate fountain, where the sunlight played on golden fish, captivated me. I couldn't hide my astonishment. The perfection of nature captured and closed behind these gates made my heart fall in love with it.

'See, Agostina,' my father chuckled, 'our daughter is impressed with trees and flowers, not knowing what a breathtaking beauty lies behind the walls of the house.'

The house was a display of wealth and power, a testament to its owner's status. And while I was not one to enjoy such things, it still managed to impress me. The guests seemed comfortable, glasses in hands, gayly engaged in sprinkled conversations. I recognised faces and moved to greet a group of young women, as etiquette required.

Flavia, a short girl with a round face and tiny eyes, wasted no time cornering me.

'They say Cornelius Scepion himself was a guest at your home recently.' Her voice was like a thumb pressing a bruise. The others all watched, waiting to see if I'd squirm. 'Was there a special reason for his visit?'

'It's difficult these days to separate rumour from truth,' I replied. 'I prefer to trust my own eyes before they betray me with age.' My attempt to avoid the trap wasn't well-received, but before Flavia could press me further, I excused myself and walked away. I could feel their stares burning into my back, their murmurs chasing after me, sharp at my heels.

'She is insufferable,' Cecilia hissed before I was too far to hear. 'Hiding behind her riddles, thinking herself clever.'

'She thinks she's so mysterious and interesting, but we're not fooled like the men she plays,' came another comment whose owner I didn't recognise, but the contempt was familiar enough.

'She's not even that beautiful,' Flavia's voice cut through impatiently. 'Soon, no one will want her, and she'll be left alone.'

Their words stung, leaving a bitter ache in my chest, but I resisted the temptation to turn back and play their game. My place wasn't here. But where then? My mother's wisdom echoed in my mind: *'When a drop of water falls into a lake, it's unidentifiable, but if it falls on a leaf, it shines like a diamond.'* I just had to find my place to shine, away from this cruel and petty world.

I saw my father engaged in a conversation with a group of men, probably members of the Senate. When he caught my gaze, he eagerly gestured for me to join them.

'Ah, Emiliy, your daughter has illuminated us with her presence,' a large old man began in a flattering tone. 'A divine beauty, my dear. The man fortunate enough to stand by your side will be truly blessed.'

'Thank you, Quint Atian,' I replied with a polite nod. 'And I would consider it an honour to stand by a good and decent man.'

My response came out sharper than intended, underlining words like *good* and *decent* as they appear to be rare qualities in people. Laughter spread among the group.

'She certainly has a sharp mind, Emiliy,' Quint Atian remarked with amusement before smoothly steering the conversation, 'And speaking of kindness, the very reason for today's event is quite something. The Prefect is quite a noble figure, isn't he? Though, I must admit, perhaps a touch too noble!'

As I listened, I sensed this new topic was something I'd rather avoid, but I couldn't excuse myself so soon. The proper thing for me to do was to remain silent. Speaking out could embarrass my father among the influential men. Yet, there was a battle within me – to stay quiet or speak my mind.

'There is no point discussing what's already done,' Atian declared, his face flushed with fervour. 'Those rioters? They're lazy complainers. Always whining: "This is missing", "That's not enough". Bah! Let them work harder, I say. Nothing in this world is free!'

'Come on, Atian, don't be so harsh,' a short man standing next to him interrupted with a chuckle. 'It was a good year. Surely, you can spare a little for others?'

Everyone's loud laughs followed.

'Don't forget, Fluvius,' Atian continued with a smirk, 'give the dog a finger, and it'll bite your hand in gratitude! My wife constantly complains we don't have enough servants, and frankly, I wouldn't mind a fresh addition under my roof – if you know what I mean.' He winked and laughed loudly, joined by the others.

I felt sick. I excused myself and stepped away from the group. What had brought me here? Why had I thought this time might be different? These people were blind, all of them – obsessed with the price of everything and the value of nothing. Did my mother really believe there was hope, that we had a mission to help those doomed souls to open their eyes? It didn't seem possible.

Feverishly, I made my way through the crowd towards the garden, desperate for air. It seemed to be the only place here that held true beauty – it was the only place I could stand to be until my family and I would leave. But as I walked, someone called for attention. There was a sudden silence in the room. It was time for the Prefect's speech.

'Friends, I'm honoured to welcome you to my home today, to celebrate with me and share in the joy that has stirred so much talk.'

As his voice filled the room, I turned around to see him. The Prefect stood on a marble step, allowing all eyes to fall upon him. He was dressed in a finely woven tunic with a deep purple stripe marking his high rank. The Prefect was a man in his prime, tall and athletic with blond hair and bright blue eyes. His presence alone exuded authority.

'Let the celebration begin,' he announced, a touch solemnly if I wasn't mistaken.

The music grew back into the fore, and the dancers moved, enchanted by the rhythm. Glasses were raised in cheers, joy settled like a warm blanket over the guests, and I ... I stood frozen, unable to make even the smallest movement. I was nearly as confused as I was days ago. I had a sudden memory, without explanation as to how or why it chose now to surface. I could see the Prefect in my mind's eye, deeply focused on parchments at his desk in an office where I had never set foot. As I tried to make something out of my own confusion, he turned suddenly, as though summoned by my thoughts, and his gaze locked onto mine. We stared at each other in a moment that stretched unexpectedly long. Dizzy and overwhelmed, I moved to the garden at nearly a run – I needed to get away.

It was a pleasant night. The sun had just been hidden, but its warmth could still be felt. The crickets sang their melodic chorus, and the scent of flowers mixed in the air. I approached a big tree and stretched my hand to touch it. My mother had often said that trees held energy. It felt good to reconnect with nature; perhaps that was what I had been missing. A sudden realisation struck me – I needed to visit the temple of the goddess Minerva, to seek inner peace and answers for everything I couldn't explain to myself.

'Forgive me,' a deep voice called, breaking the silence around me.

I let out a small scream and turned, startled. The Prefect stood just steps away.

'I hoped not to frighten you,' he said with an apologetic smile, 'but it seems I've failed.'

'It's not your fault; I was so distracted that I didn't hear you approach.' I forced a faint smile to be polite.

He looked at me for what felt like a long time – longer than what was considered socially appropriate.

'Is the feast not to your liking?' he asked with a measured tone.

'Not at all,' I replied too quickly, aware there may be consequences for having spoken so candidly – my parents would not have been happy with me. 'I mean, this feast will be remembered for years to come. I only stepped outside because I fell in love with the garden earlier and wanted to admire it again. Forgive me if I've offended you.'

'I cannot imagine you capable of offending me,' he said softly, his words hanging in the air. 'Even I find it overwhelming inside at times. This garden often offers me the peace I need.' He glanced around and took in a breath. 'It's where I come to clear my mind or find a solution to a problem.'

'Was it here that you decided to show mercy to the rebels?' I asked. I knew I was pushing my luck, but I couldn't help myself.

He smiled, though I couldn't understand why. 'No, that decision was made in my office.'

The memory of him behind his desk appeared in my mind again. I studied him quietly, sensing something deep – I felt a kindness in him, but his eyes didn't lack the sharpness of cruelty. He looked like a man at war with himself.

'Forgive me, I haven't introduced myself,' he continued. 'Beyond the title, my name is Davide Biagio.'

'Patricia, of the family Aemiliano.'

'A name as beautiful as its owner.'

Before he could continue, a servant arrived to inform him that his presence was required inside.

'It seems impossible for my absence to go unnoticed these days,' he sighed. I could sense he was reluctant to leave.

'Responsibilities and title have their price,' I replied.

'Indeed. And sometimes it's quite high ... I hope our paths cross again, Patricia.' He nodded.

'It would be an honour, Prefect.' I replied with a smile, as etiquette required.

When my parents and I finally returned home, they laughed and talked cheerfully while I was left with a storm of thoughts.

'Tomorrow I will visit the temple of Minerva,' I announced suddenly.

My parents exchanged surprised glances but didn't object.

'Take Lucretia with you, for our peace of mind,' my mother instructed me, reasonably as always.

'And a few of the other servants,' my father added, 'strong boys.'

'So it will be,' I agreed.

Once in my chambers, I sighed with relief. The day was over. I returned my jewellery to its boxes, undressed and lay down. Dreamily, I slipped into a sleep, where a voice whispered my name.

The journey to the temple was peaceful. My father's order to travel accompanied was not unreasonable; our route passed through the area where the rebellions had started. This place had become dangerous; a tough and unfair life had led people to despair. Unfortunately, their voices were not strong enough to touch the hearts of the wealthy and powerful society in the city – in their eyes, the poor were infected, and they preferred to crush them, not realising they themselves were incurably sick. Wealth could be an insidious thing, turning people into ferocious, bloodthirsty beasts, always and now, but I had hopes for a different future. The Prefect's mercy towards the rebels may very well be a mercy for the wealthy as well. Time would tell. For now I prayed the kindness wouldn't stir more problems within the ranks of the elite.

'We have arrived,' Lucretia announced with a smile, and I could tell she was excited to be out of the house.

Hidden among ancient trees just beyond the city, the temple was a haven of silence, broken only by birdsong. As I looked around, a stream caught my eye. I didn't miss the chance to dip my hand into the cold water. The refreshing power of it seemed to wash away all the tension in me. I felt ready to enter the sacred place.

Inside was dimly lit, and the air was filled with the scent of dried herbs and oils. At its centre stood the statue of Minerva, serene and majestic. I had a secret preference for her, even though I realised how wrong that was – all gods had to be respected because each one took care of people. I felt slightly ashamed of such a stupid human weakness, but I had my reasons; she was the protector of women, concerned about harmony among people and familial peace, and she was the guardian of love! Kneeling before her, I bowed my head, burdened by the weight of questions with no answers. Tears slid silently down my cheeks.

A hand gently touched my shoulder. I thought Lucretia was trying to comfort me, but when I looked up, I saw an old man in a purple toga. His face was lined with kindness, and there was a silence to him, a wisdom.

'Hello, daughter of Minerva. Are you lost?' he asked. The question felt strange yet accurate.

'No—I just …' I stammered.

'Follow me.'

Without a murmur, I stood up, made a sign to Lucretia to wait for me, and I followed him. He led me outside to the same stream, and just like I did earlier, he knelt to dip his hand as I watched in silence and expectation.

'Did you know that water holds energy?' he asked, finally breaking the somewhat awkward silence.

'Yes, my mother told me.'

'She's a wise woman,' he said, shaking the water from his hand and standing to face me. 'I see much of her in you. But I also see sadness. Tell me, what troubles you?'

It took me only a second to build the right words in my mind, but as I opened my mouth, they broke out in a scramble.

I felt somewhat odd in his presence, as if he possessed some power that broke through my social defences. Finally, the words came. 'I seek answers – for myself, for others, for my life and destiny … I don't even know if anyone will hear me or if anything will change.'

He listened patiently, waiting for me to calm before speaking. 'Sometimes, silence is the best answer. Do you know what a temple is?'

Was this one of those misleading questions with a strangely obvious answer? Confused, I instinctively gestured towards the temple behind us.

'So I was right – you have lost yourself,' he exclaimed. 'The temple is within you. To find peace, you must first know yourself. If you need to pray, you don't have to travel distances. Don't ask the gods to change the world, but to guide you in how to walk through this life.'

His words struck me – they were challenging. Did he really say I didn't have to visit the temple? This was so different and new that I couldn't keep myself from doubting, yet somehow, I felt his words held the answer I was seeking.

'Why do gods fail to help us sometimes? Why do they allow troubles to befall us?' I asked. I felt I was testing the limits of this conversation.

'They can't be responsible for human actions. They guide and teach us in their own ways, but if one does not seek or want their help, they are powerless. Just like a mother cannot prevent her child from falling, but she will always be there to help them back on their feet and encourage them to keep going forward. Gods do the same for us. We have the power to choose, yet so often, we choose wrongly.' He smiled, but there was grief on his face and a resolve in his eyes. 'No one in this world is pure and perfect, and one does not change when they are being criticised, only when being loved. Behind rage there is pain, so judge less and love more, my daughter.'

I was struck by the truth in what he said. At least his words felt true, and if they were, they were also quite sad – humankind was so smart and yet wrong. What a paradox. He interrupted my thoughts with a sudden, harsh whisper. I wondered why the low voice when there was no one around to overhear.

'I know your secret, and I'll give you some important advice. Follow it, and you'll go far.' I stared at him in shock. How could he possibly know anything about me? 'If you want to succeed, move as the turtle – steadily and slowly. Do not deviate. Your reward won't be delayed – it will be greater than any earthly treasure. But you must be strong to deserve it.'

Move as the turtle? But what was I to move towards? At that moment, I heard the crack of branches behind me.

*

Agostina and Emiliy enjoyed their late breakfast on the balcony, where the sun pleasantly caressed them. Suddenly, Clementina, one of their servants, appeared breathlessly.

'What's going on, Clementina?' Agostina asked.

'A very important guest, madam!' Clementina gasped. 'He didn't even wait for me to invite him in – or to inform you. He entered as if this were his own house. He's in the main hall now, and I'm afraid the meeting cannot be delayed.'

'Who could it be at this hour?' Emiliy asked, perplexed. 'It's not even time for lunch; is it really so urgent?'

'It's the Prefect's envoy, master,' Clementina said with timid eyes.

Agostina and Emiliy exchanged a quick glance, and both stood up from the table on the second. They had no choice but to hurry to the hall, followed by their scared servant.

A young boy with a gentle face and dark hair was waiting impatiently, a serious expression hanging on his face, no doubt for the man he represented.

'Good day,' Emiliy greeted. 'To what do we owe the honour of this visit?'

'On behalf of the Prefect, I am here to inform your daughter Patricia that he expects her consent to join him for lunch at the mansion today.'

Horror washed over the parents' faces. The Prefect's request was unexpected, and Patricia's absence was more than unlucky. Neither had anticipated an invitation of such importance. It was a delicate situation – obviously, the Prefect would be dining alone today, but neither Agostina nor Emiliy were eager to deliver the bad news.

'This is ... an incredible honour for our family, for our Patricia ...' Emiliy stammered while nervously wringing his hands. 'And we believe she would respond positively ... if only she were here.'

'At sunrise, she made her way to the temple of the goddess Minerva,' Agostina added with a composed smile, looking somewhat calmer than her husband.

'I see,' the envoy replied with an unreadable face. 'I'll inform the Prefect. Have a pleasant day.' With that, the young man was gone as swiftly as he'd appeared.

Finally alone, Emiliy began pacing back and forth.

'How did this happen, Agostina? Such bad luck! Of all people, the Prefect himself takes an interest in her, and she finds a way to avoid him! I just hope this won't weaken his interest in her.'

'Calm yourself, Emiliy,' Agostina soothed her husband. 'When something is meant to be, it finds a way. Don't waste your nerves in vain. Nothing is decided yet ... I have a good feeling about this.'

Agostina's words carried a quiet certainty.

*

Whoever was approaching, I still couldn't see their face. I turned back to the priest to continue with our conversation, but I was stunned to find myself alone. There was no sign of him – not even a sound when leaving. I stood there confused, with nothing but the memory of his words lingering in my mind.

'A wonderful day, isn't it?' The person who had been approaching was now standing right behind me.

I turned quickly and was shocked for the second time within seconds.

'Prefect?' I exclaimed. Despite myself and custom, I was staring intently at him, thinking I was mistaken.

'Are you alright? You look unwell.' He had a concerned look.

'I-I'm fine, Prefect, thank you. It's probably just from the trip. Fresh air is all I need,' I replied, trying to steady myself. 'But what are you doing here?'

My honest reaction seemed to amuse him, and a bright smile spread across his face – he looked radiant.

'I guess the same thing you're doing here.'

'I came to seek solitude and pray to the goddess.' A quiet voice within me suggested he was there for a different reason, and I just couldn't quite figure out what it was just yet.

'I also came to search for something ... but first, let me apologise if my presence has inconvenienced you.'

'Not at all,' I assured him, worried that my bluntness might not be received well a second time. 'Meeting you is always a pleasure,' I offered politely.

'What a coincidence.' He smiled again as if my answer was exactly what he'd expected to hear. 'I enjoy your company too, which is why I invited you to lunch today.'

Just when I hoped to have the situation under my control, I was again confused; meanwhile, he was standing before me and seemed to be enjoying himself.

'My apologies, Prefect, but I have no memory of receiving such an invitation.'

He laughed as I blinked in confusion. What was I missing?

'Correct,' he said smiling. 'The invitation came earlier today, but your parents kindly explained your absence and mentioned your visit to the temple. So, here we are – *meeting by chance*, which I must say, I'm quite pleased about.'

Now everything had become crystal clear: he had come to find me. The thought left me both flattered and uneasy. What did this mean for my situation? Where would it lead? Endless questions spun in my mind, but for once I decided to let myself go with the flow and see where it would take me.

I found myself amused by the thought of toying with the Prefect.

'I'm afraid fulfilling your request at this point won't be possible,' I said, allowing myself to be playful – he was kind enough.

The smile began to fade from his face, replaced by irritation and confusion.

'Of course, if you have unfinished business here, I understand, but I don't see what else would prevent us taking our lunch together,' he insisted.

'Oh yes, my work here is done, but I still fear that lunch would be impossible.' I wielded my words like a whip against his pride. Sensing the time was right, I decided to end my game before I pushed him too far.

'Because, my dear Prefect,' I continued with a smile, 'lunchtime has long since passed.'

He burst into laughter that spread across the valley. My joke had apparently pleased him. It was a relief to know he had a sense of humour. Perhaps having a conversation with him wasn't the worst idea. It was a fine line I walked – I needed to be amicable and show gratitude, and I truly didn't mind his company, but I was also aware of what he might be expecting from this, and I wasn't so sure I saw him that way.

'Don't worry, Patricia,' he said, still chuckling. 'I always think a step ahead – sometimes even two!' As he spoke, he gestured for one of his servants, who promptly stepped forwards carrying a large basket.

'I see you are well-prepared,' I replied, slightly embarrassed. 'Unfortunately, I'm not dressed appropriately for the occasion.'

He took a step closer, closing the small distance between us. I could feel his warm breath as he whispered softly, 'Your beauty, Patricia, is what stands out.'

I felt my cheeks grow warm – I hoped it wasn't visible.

We settled on a beautiful meadow, where the tall trees provided shade, their branches leaving playful gaps for the sun to filter through. The calm beauty of the place was undeniable. Davide, as he'd revealed himself to be, was intelligent and well-read – far from the man I had expected.

To my pleasant surprise, he seemed to accept me as an equal, freely discussing serious topics genuinely weighing my opinion. The formal Prefect had given way to the man beneath, to Davide – someone who made me laugh and didn't shy away from admiring me, though his gaze did linger a little too long at times.

The afternoon slipped by, and as the sun dipped low, we prepared to leave. Before parting ways, Davide stepped a little too close again. 'To enjoy your company was a pleasure I'm tempted to repeat,' he whispered softly.

I stepped back to keep a polite distance. 'It was an honour to have my presence deemed worthy by you, Prefect,' I replied with a flat tone, but I intended to show less emotion so he wouldn't get ahead of himself.

As I walked away, I could feel his gaze burning into my back. His thoughts were easy to read, and what he wanted from me, I couldn't give him. He wasn't the one I was waiting for – I knew that deep in my heart.

On the way back home, my dear Lucretia analysed the situation, but her conclusion didn't feel helpful. My mother's desired to find me a match, and soon the Prefect would be the best candidate of them all. I'd discovered someone interesting behind his title, but to go with him wouldn't be staying true to myself, though I couldn't deny it would make things easier.

'My dear ... what I saw was a man, not the Prefect, and he adores you! He was observing every word of yours, every gesture. His desire contains much more than just lust. Trust me, Patricia – I know these things. That man is at your feet!' Lucretia winked playfully.

Back home, I knew I had to face worried parents. My father didn't even greet me as usual.

'Where have you been? Did you dine with the goddess herself?' His tone was sharp. I rarely saw him behave this way with me.

'Shame on you, Emiliy! Where is your respect for the gods?' my mother snapped and silenced him with a look.

'No, father,' I said calmly, 'but I did have lunch with the Prefect himself.'

His eyes widened in disbelief. 'How ...?'

'It happened that he also visited the temple,' I tried to explain as casually as I could; I knew my parents, and I knew this situation would only raise expectations I wasn't ready to meet.

'Yes, a very *coincidental* meeting,' my father laughed. 'Don't think you can fool me. We're the ones who told the envoy where the Prefect could find you.'

'It doesn't matter, Emiliy,' my mother said more gently this time. 'Can't you see she's tired? Let her rest. We can discuss this tomorrow.'

To my surprise, she urged me to leave, and I didn't wait for a second invitation. All I wanted was the comfort of my bed and peace so I could put my thoughts together.

*

The stables were one of my favourite places. I loved watching the horses. I had a favourite – a magnificent creature whose grace, colour, and posture made him the most beautiful in my eyes. Being around the horses always calmed me, as though they absorbed my tension and replaced it with tranquillity.

'Do you mind some company?'

A voice startled me, and I turned to see my mother standing quietly beside me.

'Of course not.'

The day before, I'd left my parents with more questions than answers about the recent events. My mother had given me space to gather my thoughts, but now the time for answers had come.

'It's peaceful here,' she said, gazing at the horses standing quietly. 'I can see why you love it.'

'Yes,' I said, 'it's far safer here than anywhere filled with people.'

She chuckled softly. 'Why do you think that?'

'Because everything in nature happens naturally, even an act of apparent aggression would be without malice. A person, on the other hand, seeks too much with their actions.'

'You're right,' she said, 'we're small and insignificant, yet armed for a war against nature itself. You see so clearly the silliness of humankind, and it weighs on you, though none of it is your fault. You are pure as a tear … that's why the gods chose you. Do you understand now how important your role is? And why it's so vital to keep our family secret? But remember, the greatest lesson on your journey is to master yourself. For whoever does not master themselves is a slave, no matter how powerful they may be.'

She smiled at me and ran her fingers through my hair.

'Mother ... I want to tell you what I experienced right before meeting the Prefect yesterday,' I said. Sensing I had her full attention, I went right into my story about the old man from the temple who had vanished without a sound. As I spoke, I realised how surreal it sounded, even to my own ears. Yet my mother, as always, was ready with the answer.

'Patricia,' she spoke gently, 'that was no ordinary man. He was a god in human form, sent to meet you, to help you discover yourself and guide you to your path. Trust what he told you. As for the Prefect, his presence was no coincidence either. The great forces brought him to that sacred place so that your paths would cross. Everything has a purpose, even if it isn't immediately clear. Resist as you may, the stars have already written your destiny. The less you fight it, the easier it will become to understand. This connection with him is meant to be, and when you accept that, everything will begin to make sense.'

Tears filled my eyes. Was I really a puppet in the hands of the gods? That kind of rigid destiny didn't feel very appealing; I wanted happiness, but it seemed I had to sacrifice a lot to have it, including my dreams of love. Was the Prefect really what I was meant to see?

'But I'm ready for love and—'

'We rarely know when we are truly ready, my daughter,' my mother interrupted, still with her soft voice. 'There is still much to learn, especially about love.'

She kissed my forehead and wiped away my tears.

*

'Are you excited?' Lucretia asked me with an enthused voice. She was everything I wasn't at this very moment.

'I'm nervous and not in the good sense,' I replied.

She caressed me reassuringly. 'You know I'll always be with you. Whatever you go through – I'll be there!' She'd said exactly what I needed to hear.

Today, we were expecting yet another visit. What set this occasion apart wasn't the visit itself but the visitor. The Prefect was coming to our house

Since our 'coincidental' meeting at the temple of Minerva, my family received a notice for his visit. From the moment the letter arrived, tension and excitement had filled the house. Everyone saw a reason for celebration, but also seemed uneasy around me, as though I were an unwieldy animal that might start breaking things at any moment. To me, the visit was not a joy but a reason for grief.

As we reached the doors to the big hall, I stopped walking without realising. I felt Lucretia's hand on my back gently pushing me forward. Only seconds later, as I entered the hall where my presence was expected, I felt my parents' eyes lock on me. I took my place and had nothing else to do but wait.

The arrival of our guest was announced, and just a moment later, he stood before us. To my surprise, the Prefect seemed as nervous as I was.

'It is an honour to welcome you to our modest home.' My father greeted him first.

'I'm pleased to be here today, especially seeing as I've come with a purpose,' the Prefect said.

I studied his face and noticed something I hadn't expected to see – at least not from him, not now, and certainly not because of me. But there it was, unmistakable. He was beginning to fall in love.

The Prefect took a deep breath. 'I'll speak directly – I've come to ask for your blessing for Patricia to become my wife, for she already owns my heart.'

The words hung in the air, electrifying the hall. My parents exclaimed enthusiastically.

'What an unexpected surprise!' My father's excitement was almost childlike. He barely contained himself, as though the offer had been made to him rather than me. I could understand his reasons – this union would secure our family's position. Was I selfish to think that such motives meant nothing to me?

'Let's hear our daughter,' my mother reminded everyone with a calm smile; she'd always been able to conceal her tension well.

All eyes turned to me, but one gaze burned hotter than the rest – it was his. The Prefect's eyes had been fixed on me since he entered the hall. They were not the eyes I saw in my dreams. They didn't belong to the one I longed for. Yet, what did that matter now, when the power to shape my fate was no longer in my hands?

He awaited my answer, my favour, my smile. Before me stood not the title, the authority, of the Prefect, but the man beneath, a man in love. They say love could make people burn. But in my case, there wasn't even a spark. Davide carried the fire for both of us, and for now, that would be enough. Still, how long could such an imperfection be sustained before it consumed us both?

There was at least something in him that impressed me, a little grain of kindness buried deep within his heart. That was the only reason on which I based my answer.

'I agree to be your wife.' My voice was flat and emotionless; there wasn't even a smile. I did what was expected of me.

Later on, while the rest of the household celebrated with wine and a feast in our honour, he approached me. Taking my hand gently, he kissed it and whispered, 'You will be the happiest woman. I swear it.'

I believed him. I felt sincerity in his words.

But a quiet voice in the back of my mind added, *Yes, but not with you.*

*

The end of the hot summer was coming, but the truth was that it never really went – we enjoyed the warmth almost all year round, but the evenings became cooler. Time seemed to slip through my fingers, and I was helpless to stop it. I dreamed of having wings like the wild birds I often watched from my balcony – wings that could carry me far from this place, away from the upcoming wedding, away from the Prefect … and closer to someone whose face and name I didn't know yet but whose existence I clung to with desperate hope.

*

I was nervous. Today my union with the Prefect was going to be announced publicly. My thoughts didn't let me sleep, and by early dawn, I was already on the balcony, watching the sunrise and waiting for Lucretia.

'Good morning.' Her cheerful greeting rang out clearly as she entered my chambers.

I managed a smile, but I didn't need to pretend in front of her.

'Don't be miserable …' she urged. 'Let's decide on the clothes and the jewellery.' Her suggestion was meant to comfort me, but suddenly, an idea sparked in my mind. I felt my eyes grow wide as it took hold.

'There it is! The excitement I was hoping for,' she continued.

'No,' I said, lowering my voice, 'I have a much better idea, my dear Lucretia – and you will accompany me.'

I could see on her face that she didn't like this sudden shift in conversation. Before I could explain, I could already see the disapproval in her eyes. She suspected – correctly – that whatever I had in mind would be far from acceptable, especially on such an important day.

'Patricia, please,' she began with a pleading voice. 'Let's not get into trouble. The event has to go smoothly today, and I promise we can do whatever you want tomorrow, but not—'

'It's decided,' I interrupted her, and she knew me well enough to know it was too late to try and convince me otherwise. 'Don't be a coward,' I teased her. 'No one will notice. Today the market will be full of goods from across the sea. Imagine how wonderful it will be to see everything! I'm going crazy in here, and that would certainly cheer me up. It'll only be for a little while – we'll return before anyone even realises we're gone.'

My enthusiasm grew along with her anxiety. I grabbed a cloak for myself and practically forced one around Lucretia's shoulders.

'Follow me.' I grabbed her hand as she reluctantly did what she was told. I heard her mutter a prayer under her breath.

The market was more crowded than I'd ever seen it. People swarmed like bees, making it difficult to move. The air was filled with the rich aromas of spices, seafood, and delicacies, along with the lively chatter of traders and buyers. The stalls invitingly displayed fabrics, jewels, and exotic goods. My head turned from side to side, trying not to miss anything. These markets always thrilled me – it felt as though I was touching pieces of a world I had yet to explore.

We stopped in front of a crowd of people, mostly because we were blocked from moving forward. Curious,

I tiptoed to see why everyone had gathered, and at the centre I saw a tiny wooden stage.

'A puppet theatre,' I said to Lucretia, who couldn't see much.

A man behind a curtain was making the dolls move, which caused a wave of children's laughter. Their parents, too, smiled at the simple joy of the performance.

I tried to follow the story the man was telling.

'… and the beautiful lady was so grateful to the boy who had saved her from the evil ruler who sought to force her into marriage. Their love was instant, and nothing could stop them from being happy …'

'Enough of this,' I said as I pulled Lucretia's hand and went forward. I didn't want to stay and listen to this delusion, this lie. Why teach children to believe in something that almost never happens in real life – Love? I felt the bitterness of disappointment. My good mood evaporated with this slap from reality.

I moved on with Lucretia following silently, but after a few steps, something caught my eye again. It was a small stall, seemingly no different than the others. The woman behind it was old, and she didn't have any buyers and wasn't calling out to passersby. I, on the other hand, was drawn right in. By what? I couldn't say, but this only drew me in more.

'Do you see anything you like?' Lucretia asked breathlessly – I'd moved to the stall rather quickly and she had to run to keep up.

'She's looking for something special!' the woman of the stall cut in.

Both Lucretia and I looked at her in surprise. She had grey hair and extraordinary eyes – they were so calm, so still.

'Don't worry, child,' she murmured as she searched for something, 'I have exactly what you need.'

Lucretia glanced at me nervously.

'Here it is!' The old woman held out her arm to me, and from her cupped hand, a small pendant dropped into my palm.

It wasn't luxurious, and the way it moved made it look so animated. It was captivating.

'It's beautiful,' I said, enchanted, and I could feel Lucretia's piercing gaze on me. She must have thought I was going crazy – she knew I had jewellery more valuable than this.

'I told you I knew what you needed,' the old woman laughed cheerfully.

'Patricia, we need to go,' Lucretia reminded me, and I knew she was right. 'Please!'

'How much do you want for it?' I asked.

The woman just smiled and looked at me for a long while, at least it felt like a long while.

'It's yours, child. Take it. Let it bring you joy,' she replied kindly.

'Just like that? In return for nothing?' I was surprised. She was here to trade for her bread. 'Nothing in this world is free.'

'You're right, but sometimes we've already paid without realising. Consider it a gift from an old woman.'

It was now Lucretia's turn to grab my hand impatiently. I had no more time left to figure out the mystery I thought might be hiding here. I held tight to the pendant and nodded gratefully to the old woman.

We quickly merged with the crowd, but my curiosity made me glance back. I looked back to see nothing aside from neighboring stalls, swarming people and shifting crowds. The pendant rest in my hand, but where it had come from was gone.

Back home, as Lucretia adjusted my toga, I studied the pendant. The delicate golden leaves engraved on it formed a peculiar shape. Was it a letter? An *M* perhaps, though my imagination could have been playing tricks on me.

*

My life had changed, but it was about to change even more.

Some things remained the same – like my dreams, for example. I still couldn't see the owner of the voice whispering my name, and whenever I tried to answer, I woke up. The little pendant was always with me, which Lucretia found amusing. She claimed that it had no value seeing as it was given for free. But to me, its value was beyond measure, though I could not explain why.

People's attitudes towards me changed with the upcoming wedding. No one dared to openly mock me anymore. Even the girls who'd once envied and gossiped about me now offered their friendly services, but I would still overhear their whispers, accusing me of waiting for the most advantageous proposal. They mistakenly associated my name with a thirst for wealth and power, but none of them knew me well enough to know otherwise. Convincing them wasn't worth my effort either. How could they understand when they only valued money and status? No one, apart from my mother and Lucretia, knew the truth of my inner pain. As if all that wasn't enough, I was facing another unavoidable change.

I sat in the garden, letting the sun warm my shoulders as I held the little pendant in my hands and studied how the light played on its surface.

Two hands covered my eyes suddenly.

'I know it's you, Lucretia,' I laughed.
'But you were frightened for a moment – admit it.'
'Not at all.'
'I'll catch you off guard one day.' She was a sweet, little devil.

Despite my mood brightening up around her, I couldn't keep my smile up.

'What's wrong?'

I sighed, unsure of how to begin. When I finally met her gaze, she frowned in concern.

'It's the wedding night,' I admitted hesitantly. 'I don't know what to … how do …' I just stopped there, knowing she would have understood enough.

To my surprise, Lucretia burst into laughter. It was my turn to frown. I couldn't see what was so amusing about my problem.

'You're afraid of the easiest part,' she said, barely catching her breath.

Whatever the expression on my face was, it made her stop and look at me more seriously.

'When haven't I helped you? Don't worry! But this isn't the right place for such a conversation. Your chambers would be more appropriate.'

She practically leapt up and hurried back to the house, leaving me confused. Unless the trees would mock me, I could see no good reason why we couldn't continue our conversation in the garden.

I allowed myself a few more moments of delight in the sun before finally following her.

When I reached my chambers, I had the odd feeling we were sharing a secret, and as I opened the door, things felt even odder. I froze, covering my mouth with my hands. Lucretia was there waiting, but she was dressed in a nearly transparent dressing gown with a deep neckline reaching almost to her belly button, with slits revealing her long, slender legs.

I felt my face grow hot from the unexpected sight; meanwhile, Lucretia giggled at my discomfort.

'With the right outfit, you won't need to do much – your man will do the rest,' she said playfully, but I was not in the mood for jokes.

'I could never wear that.'

'The garment is just for a moment; you will almost immediately be left without it.' With a single quick motion, she let the gown fall to the floor and stood completely naked in front of me. I could see how she owned her beauty – she could easily use it as a weapon. Then, just as swiftly, she slipped back into her toga and sat on the bed, gesturing for me to join her.

Reluctantly, I sat down, feeling more defeated than reassured.

Lucretia's tone softened. 'I know it's hard to let someone get so close to you ... but we are women, and sooner or later we must.'

Her words stung. In my mind, the approaching intimacy could have been so beautiful – a moment when love was shared between two souls. And I had sworn that my body would belong only to someone who loved my soul. I'd believed I had the luxury of free will. How naive.

Lucretia continued as disappointment and fear swelled within me:

'A man's pleasure isn't always the same as a woman's, but whether we are slaves or masters, in bed, we are all equals. Be confident, meet passion with passion, and soon you may find a way to enjoy it.'

Her hand brushed my hair gently, but her words left me hollow. I was to marry a man I didn't love. To give him my body. To share my life with him. I was no master of my fate. I didn't feel like anyone's equal – I was a slave.

And yet ... I couldn't ignore the feeling that destiny had tied me to the Prefect for a reason. He had appeared in one of my visions, and perhaps – just perhaps – this was a small sign of hope.

*

That night, I was exhausted, yet I'd cried myself to sleep, only to be woken by a nightmare. It was still dark as I blinked up at the ceiling, having just managed to calm myself. The dream was fairly abstract and not even terrible, and this was precisely what terrified me. I was running down the stairs of a narrow corridor. The steps seemed endless. I kept going, breathless, until I wasn't sure if I was running upwards or downwards. Doors appeared on either side of me. I was certain they hadn't been there before. I instinctively wanted to open one of them, desperate for escape, but suddenly I understood that I wasn't running from something – I was trying to run towards something, someone. I was seeking *him*.

I kept running. I wanted to call up his image in my mind, and maybe I could have if I'd ever seen him. The air was coming out of my chest in ragged gasps, and panic started overwhelming me. This place, so vile in its silence, a silence disturbed only by the echo of my footsteps, was leading me nowhere and to no one. A feeling of loneliness unlike anything I'd felt crept inside me. I woke up drenched in sweat with tears falling from my eyes again.

After the initial shock of the dream had warn off, the silence became unbearable for me. I couldn't stay alone. I needed Lucretia.

I left my chambers and hurried to her room. I didn't like to roam the house at night; there was something in the darkness that still frightened me, just like when I was a child – I couldn't seem to grow out of it.

I reached the door of her room and knocked. There was no answer, of course. I pushed the door half opened, trying not to make a noise, but I found her bed empty. Puzzled, I decided to check the kitchen next, but a sound coming from outside made me change my decision. Someone was moving in the garden. I hurried to get closer, but I struggled to recognise the figure in the darkness. After a moment, I lost them from my sight. Whoever it was, they'd slipped fast into the stables. One thing was for sure, I had achieved the desired goal of getting my mind off my dream. Now I was burning with curiosity about what was going on here, and I couldn't return to my chambers before I satisfied myself with an answer.

I crossed the garden at a run and opened the door to the stables as silently as possible. I looked around, but all I saw were horses that I'd woken up, pushing their frustration through their lips and thudding their hooves into the ground. A squeaking sound made me turn around. I'd forgotten about the small room used by the servants who tended to the animals. I looked over, and there did seem to be someone inside.

I held my breath and crouched by the door. A small crack provided me with a slit through which I could see, not much, but enough. I saw what had caused the squeaking sound. It was a chair, pulled from its place to accommodate one of the servants. I recognised him – he looked after my favourite horse. But he wasn't alone – Lucretia was there.

Everything happened so fast, and I seemed unable to look away. She lifted the skirts of her dress and wrapped her legs around him, and he gently ran his hands over her thighs, caressing her skin. For a moment, they stared at each other – it was one of the most intimate things I'd ever seen. And then, as if an invisible wall between them had disappeared, they crushed their bodies into each other. Fingers ran through hair and pulled away clothing. His grip left marks on her skin, but it didn't seem to cause her pain; on the contrary, she pressed herself harder into him. Their lips merged, then separated to kiss other parts of their hot bodies, and then they found each other again.

I stood up and ran away from there. I couldn't be a witness to this moment meant only for two. But mostly, what I couldn't accept was the fact that soon the same thing would be expected from me. I wasn't capable of doing it, not with the Prefect!

*

The Wedding Day.
I woke up, but I kept my eyes closed. They felt unusually heavy, as if the long night failed to offer enough rest, but also, the tears on my eyelids hadn't yet dried and held my eyes mercifully shut. I didn't want to wake up. I didn't want this day to begin.

A gentle touch caressed my hair, fingers playing with it and brushing lightly against my skin. It was pleasant until a sudden thought struck me – who was in my bed?

I opened my eyes. A face stared back, so shockingly beautiful I almost screamed. Golden hair fell softly over her shoulders, milky-white skin, thick pink lips, and eyes – oh, the eyes! They grabbed me, pulling me into them, from the moment our gaze locked. I'd never seen her before, at least, not in the flesh – not in my bed. I'd only seen images, artwork, a statue in her temple. Juno, the goddess and patroness of marriage, was holding me in her eyes.

She gave me the most wonderful smile, but I was unable to answer with the same. Frozen in fear, I clutched at the covers, seeking to hide under them and save myself.

I knew why she was here – there was a reason for her to be angry. But she acted as if nothing was wrong, humming a tune while her fingers began plaiting my hair.

'You will be such a beautiful bride!' she exclaimed as her fingers moved quickly through the braiding. Her behaviour reminded me of the calm just before a storm hits.

'What do you want?' The words barely made it past my trembling lips.

She paused and looked at me, her eyes burning inside myself.

'What do *you* want? There must be a reason for you to violate the rules. Tell me before I decide your fate!'

She was right – the gods were always right. They wanted only good for us, but we so often disrespected them by ignoring them. But I was being forced into this marriage with a man I did not love – I was searching for someone else.

'I understand,' she said softly, though I hadn't spoken a word. 'Still, that doesn't change the fact that you sinned deliberately.'

Her fingers were no longer moving gently on my hair. Instead, her fist grabbed a bunch of it together, pulling it roughly as her beautiful face distorted in frustration and anger. She was deciding how to punish me.

'I'll give you a wedding gift,' she announced flatly. 'Though you haven't honoured me, I will show mercy. The gods offer second chances. We forgive … sometimes.'

I listened, uncertain of what to expect. Suddenly, she pulled my hair to bring my face within a breath of hers. I stared into her eyes, so closely I could truly see them – a whole universe reflected there, stars, galaxies, and eternity itself. Her other hand slid across my breasts until she found my heart. A piercing pain made me moan, and then it vanished as suddenly as it had started.

'Your heart will remain untouched by passion, unmoved by desire, until you find the one you truly seek. You may know loyalty, you may know duty, you may even know love in some of its forms, but you will not know the love that sets souls alight – this will remain beyond your grasp until fate decides you are ready.'

I opened my eyes, breathing heavily, completely alone. I pulled myself up into a sitting position and ran my fingers through my hair and then felt my chest. My heart was where it was meant to be, beating rhythmically. I sighed. What kind of a dream was that?

The doors opened and Lucretia entered with a bright smile.

'I'm glad to see you already awake! I thought I'd have to drag you out of bed,' she teased as she sat beside me.

'Lucretia …' I moaned, leaning my head against her shoulder.

'What's wrong?'

'I had the worst dream. I was so afraid, and she was so angry, and it hurt …'

'She? Who are you talking about?'

'Juno. I dreamed of her.' I almost cried at the memory of it, but Lucretia only laughed as her worry seemed to fade.

'Oh, my dear, there is nothing to fear. She was here to bless you,' she explained as if I didn't know that was Juno's typical role, but the dream, the tone, the fear, was all different. 'Come now, it's time to prepare you.'

It had felt more like a punishment than a blessing. Was it really a dream? Only one thing was certain: I'd broken the tradition of paying the goddess respect with a ritual the night before the wedding day. But I didn't seek a blessing from the gods – I didn't want luck or happiness for this union with the Prefect as it was nothing more than a facade for me.

As my mother and Lucretia took care of preparing me for the wedding ceremony, I realised that despite my hopes and prayers over the past few months, nothing had prevented this day from coming. Was there any hope? Hope that there could still be happy days ahead of me, a time with a smile on my face instead of tears? A time when I'd be next to the man I seemed only capable of dreaming about – my soul mate. Yes, there was hope – I had left was hope!

Wind brought clouds, heavy with rain, which threatened to pour out like a flood. The sky wanted to cry with me. But even so, the sacred alliance, meant to be kept for a lifetime, practically indestructible, was made, and there was no turning back for me.

The celebration after the ceremony was a spectacular event – nobody had expected anything less. People would talk about it for years to come. Magnificent, abundant and luxurious, it wasn't to my taste at all, but I had to admit that I'd never attended anything like it before. And all of it was in my honour.

People took turns talking to us, greeting us, expressing their admiration; it was way too overwhelming for me, but not for my now husband. Davide didn't leave my side even for a moment – he seemed scared, as though I might run away. I wouldn't have, but I wanted to.

The day had turned into night, but the celebration continued on in force. I was sitting with a glass of wine in hand, sipping thirstily, not because I was enjoying it but because I wanted to let it have its effect on me, to blur my consciousness, at least this once. But a few moments later, a hand took mine, loosened my fingers and took my glass, setting it on the table. I didn't even turn my head to look at him – I knew who it was. He held my hand and leaned closer to whisper in my ear, 'Come with me.'

I obeyed, hoping the wine had been enough. His hand wrapped mine gently. I could feel his skin, warm and soft, his goodwill, his love. But I myself did not feel anything. He led me through the grand halls to a quiet room far from the noise. The room was light and warm. Davide stood behind me and gently moved my hair aside, softly running his fingers along my shoulders and across my back.

'This is our room,' he whispered. 'Here I will fall asleep and wake up next to you. If you only knew … how happy that makes me.'

I felt his hands on my breasts, his lips touching my neck. My dress fell to the ground with one quick movement of his. I remained still, barely breathing. He lifted me up in his arms and led me to the bed. Every touch of his was sensual and gentle, but somehow it didn't make a difference to the way I felt. I closed my eyes and waited for everything to finish …

*

I woke up yet again in his bed – I still felt reluctant to call it ours. Davide was already gone, no doubt consumed by his many responsibilities. His day always began early, which worked to my advantage – I could spend these quiet moments pretending I was still in my family home.

The door opened, and a familiar face appeared – Lucretia. Her presence made it easy to maintain my illusion. I smiled at her, grateful that hers was the first face I saw as I woke up. She gave me a sense of home wherever we were, and now, more than ever, I relied on her.

'Good morning, my dear,' she greeted me with a warm smile, but it still felt different than it had at home – she was adjusting to this new life too. Still, there was a flicker of mischief in her expression. 'There's something interesting I'd like to share with you – unless you'd rather keep to yourself?'

'No, I won't stay a second longer in this room. Let's go to the garden, and you can tell me what you know.'

'Maybe it's better to tell you first,' she said, and her smile widened slightly. 'Then you might prefer to go somewhere else.' I knew her look well.

'All right, I'm all ears …' I replied, intrigued.

She lowered her voice and sat on the bed next to me.

'The servants here gossip so much – you can learn a lot if you know how and whom to ask. I tried to blend in, and word by word, I discovered something. There's a secret tunnel – a tunnel – in the library on the second floor. I thought you'd like that – a little adventure to explore our new home.' Her eyes sparkled with excitement, and she looked almost impatient.

'A secret tunnel?' I repeated. 'Who would need one, and why?' My curiosity was challenged, and as always, it had to be satisfied. My new home was so grand and overwhelming compared to the relatively modest home I grew up in, and it still felt unwelcoming to me. Several days had passed since the wedding, and though Lucretia and I had explored most of the house, I still felt as if I could get lost at any moment. The mansion was filled with unnecessary and unused rooms, each decorated with items that seemed to exist only to collect dust. The Prefect himself had no time to enjoy his possessions, and yet he owned this and several other properties.

I couldn't understand how one could have such an insatiable desire for more, even when one already had everything. To me, anything beyond what was necessary was wasteful – a vice, perhaps even a sin, especially if it wasn't shared. In this world I knew, there was no equality.

Some people were surrounded by splendour and craved more while others lived in misery, struggling just to survive. Still, I was determined to make a difference. Having the position of the Prefect's wife, something I had never wanted, I at least carried some influence.

We were walking down the corridor that led to the library when we came across Maurizio, the Prefect's counsellor. He was a small elderly man with eyes so grey that they seemed almost transparent. His thin lips made him look as though he had none. In a way, he looked a bit like a snake, but perhaps that was too virile a comparison. There was something that made me feel uneasy around him, something that made me glad I wasn't alone. I didn't like him, and it was clear the feeling was mutual. Yet, oddly, I was sure I'd seen him before – not at some event, but somewhere else. I had the same nagging sensation I'd felt when I first met the Prefect.

Maurizio stopped to greet us as manners required.

'Good day,' he said with a polite bow, offering a passable smile. I returned the gesture. I had no interest in turning this accidental meeting into a conversation, but he persisted with a deceptively kind tone. 'We haven't had the chance to speak since you became the Prefect's lawful wife. Tell me, how does it feel to be the rightful owner of all this?' He gestured around us to the mansion.

His daring question didn't match the seemingly obedient and humble expression that he was trying to present. Beneath his words, I sensed envy and malice. I wasn't expecting such blatant impertinence, but his question only confirmed my suspicions about him. From the start, I'd felt he would bring nothing but trouble.

'I hope my answer won't disappoint you,' I replied coldly, keeping my tone just pleasant enough, 'but I don't feel myself as the owner.' I hoped my response would make him uncomfortable, or at least second guess overstepping again.

Maurizio chuckled. It was mechanical, and felt bigger than the moment called for.

'Oh, don't be modest. Give yourself a little time – you'll find it's easy to get used to life's finer things.'

I forced a final strained smile, but I knew our little war had only started. Maurizio was like a predator circling his prey, waiting for the right moment to assert his dominance.

'Well, I won't keep you,' he said as the silence between us stretched awkwardly. 'I have important tasks to attend – best not to keep the Prefect waiting.' He bowed again and walked away.

As soon as he was out of our sight, Lucretia let out a sigh of relief.

'That man is utterly dreadful,' she said, and I nodded in agreement.

'Maybe he's good at his job – that's likely why the Prefect trusts him; otherwise, he'd have been dismissed by now.' I was thoughtful for a moment. 'Did you notice where he came from?'

'The library,' she said. I waited for her to follow my train of thought. Her eyes widened as she began to piece things together. 'You think he's using the secret tunnel?'

'I don't know – we don't even know what it's for or if the Prefect is aware of it as well. It's not uncommon for houses like this to have secret escape routes. All the same, something about this smells.' The thoughts my mind ran with were more than terrible. If any of them were true, the snake of a man was indeed venomous, and the Prefect was keeping him right next to him. I didn't love the Prefect, but I couldn't allow this to continue. I opened the door to the library and stepped inside, Lucretia following behind.

It was by far the biggest collection I'd ever seen. Shelves lined every wall, filled with the world's greatest treasure – knowledge. In an instant I already knew this room would become my second favourite place here, after the garden. For a moment, I stood in awe, nearly forgetting the purpose of our visit.

'I'll search one side, and you can take the other,' Lucretia suggested, gently reminding me of our mission. I nodded and began inspecting the shelves, running my fingers lightly over the dusty spines of untouched parchments, wondering what secrets they concealed. Behind me, Lucretia hummed a melody, a nervous habit of hers I recognised well. My own heart raced with the thrill of discovery.

After some time sifting through random documents and running my hand along any vaguely peculiar surface, my attention was drawn to a carving – a crescent moon engraved into the wood of one of the shelves. It seemed out of place.

'Have you found anything?' Lucretia's sudden question startled me. I jumped, clutching my chest with one hand while steadying myself against the shelf with the other.

'No, but you nearly scared me to death.'

'Ha! I told you that someday I'd manage to surprise you,' she chuckled triumphantly, but her tone then changed. 'Patricia, look, I think …'

I followed her gaze, now locked on the same crescent moon. Lucretia didn't think twice before she traced her fingers over it, pressing down in various places until one yielded a soft click that echoed throughout the room.

'We've found it,' I whispered as the shelf shifted, revealing a narrow opening just wide enough for someone to slip through.

The excitement in me had reached heights that I'd not experienced for some time. Lucretia came over to me, and I took her hand and walked into the tunnel. She was afraid, and her grip on my hand was as tight as a child's. At the entrance, a torch lay waiting, still warm – clear evidence that the tunnel had recently been used. We lit it and the dim light revealed a narrow corridor; it smelled of stale air and damp stone.

The deeper we went in, the harder it was to summon courage, especially with Lucretia trembling behind me. The light from the torch wasn't enough to completely illuminate the tunnel, but it fortunately wasn't necessary to see the next thing that caught my attention, a small beam of light coming from a crack in the wall. Handing the torch to Lucretia, I pressed a finger to my lips, signing silence, and bent closer to look through the small hole. The sight on the other side nearly made me gasp aloud – the Prefect's office. Inside, Davide sat at his desk, his expression tense as Maurizio stood before him. He seemed to be having difficulty persuading Davide into something. His face was reddened from anger, eyes narrowed like a predator stalking its victim, with a forced smile to try and cover it all.

His words could barely reach me, so I pressed my ear against the hole instead.

'… a woman always makes a man happier,' Maurizio chuckled, but the mockery was transparent to me and apparently to Davide. 'But it also distracts a man. Your job requires full dedication, especially now … a long break might not be wise.'

Davide's voice sliced through the air.

'Let me remind you, Counsellor, that you advise on matters of state, not my personal life. My decisions are my own.' It was clear that the limits of Davide's patience had been reached. Maurizio, however, didn't flinch. His persistence, whether out of arrogance or strategy, was unbreakable.

'Of course, of course. Forgive me if I misspoke. I only meant to suggest a shorter break rather than a long one. I understand your need to enjoy her beautiful face …'

Davide's hands slammed down on the desk. He was no longer sitting. The counsellor, however, didn't seem frightened by this outburst of emotion.

'How dare you speak so freely about my wife.' His voice was ice. 'She has a name and title. Showing disrespect can lead to serious consequences!' Every word had been strained through his jaw, tight with anger.

Maurizio skillfully played his deep regret, placing a remorse mask on his face, which might have misled someone else, but not me. I could see right through him and his wretchedness.

'Forgive me, my dear Prefect. The gods know I meant no harm. My loyalty to you is stronger than the love for my own life.' He lowered his head obediently.

I stepped back from the wall. I had seen and heard enough, and I already knew what kind of person I was facing. Maurizio's malice was no longer a suspicion but a certainty. I gestured to Lucretia and we moved forward; it was important to find out what other parts of the mansion were being watched by the Counsellor. My thoughts wandered chaotically as we stepped carefully through the tunnel. So it was true – Davide really loved me. This love was unshared, and his attempts to make me love him back were doomed, but he was worthy of admiration – he respected me unconditionally. Sometimes, this was enough for a good start. I owed him the same dedication – I wouldn't allow the counsellor to continue to poison him. I was going to expose him.

Ahead, another beam of light made itself known. As before, I stopped to peek through – the view was of our private chambers. I pressed my lips together, trying to hold the overwhelming feeling of disgust I had for this coward Maurizio. Did I need to move on? Whatever I found from here on could only torment me more. I turned to Lucretia, who was looking over her shoulder, clearly anxious.

'I'm ready to leave,' I whispered.

On the way back, we stepped more boldly, and soon we found ourselves in the bright and spacious library.

'Let's never do that again,' Lucretia pleaded as she exhaled with relief.

'It won't be necessary, dear,' I said flatly. I couldn't let my emotions out just yet, although I felt as if I were going to burst into tears, not from sadness but disbelief about the problems I found myself facing now.

'What did you see?' she asked in concern, now that she could clearly see my expression.

'Everything,' I replied. 'It's worse than we imagined. This place isn't a home, Lucretia. It's a maze of secrets, filled with people we can't trust.'

She took my hand. 'I'll keep you safe.' I knew her vow was a pure and honest one, but could both of us fight against this?

Evening came, and I watched the stars from the balcony of my chambers. I heard the doors opening, and I knew it was Davide. His hands embraced me gently and I shivered.

'It's cold here. Let's get inside,' he offered with a soft voice.

I knew it wasn't the night breeze making me tremble; I just couldn't teach my body to get used to my husband's closeness. I followed him inside, and after a few steps, he stopped and faced me with a glowing smile. I felt confused, as if I had missed something.

'The day is finally over, and I admit that this fact has never made me so happy as it's making me now.' He gently kissed me, but my lips remained motionless to his touch. 'I've planned a surprise for you – we're going on a journey tomorrow morning.'

The news was not a surprise to me, but I couldn't afford to show that just yet, not before deciding when and how to tell Davide about my discovery.

'That's a wonderful idea,' I replied as excitedly as I could make myself look.

'I will do anything to see your smile,' he said, kissing me again, this time pressing his lips to mine, making his passion known.

*

The summer season was slowly fading, slipping into autumn. Every type of weather had its charm for those who had eyes for it. The mornings were crisp now as we travelled – the sun just beginning to rise, its rays not yet reaching the ground to warm it. We'd been moving about for some time, and we were ready for our trip back home. Surprisingly, I had found myself enjoying Davide's company more than I had expected.

He'd planned our journey in such a way that he could show me all he governed, which now, by extension, was also mine. Despite all the properties and riches, I wasn't impressed. Large mansions, lavish rooms filled with expensive yet unused items – this parade of wealth only whispered of vanity, and even worse – an illusion. But Davide had certain becoming qualities, a potential I believed I could nurture. I sensed his inner struggle – an instinct to be humane and kind, which often would get overruled by the firm hand he was expected to show.

I found myself yet again overwhelmed by the beauty of a space when visiting the estate by the sea, which quickly became my favourite place. It was serene, secure, and welcoming, just like coming home. Davide was happy to finally see me pleased. I didn't have words to explain, even to myself, the way I felt at this place.

All too soon we left and returned to what was now my home, but instead of relief, a sudden wave of dizziness overtook me as we stepped inside.

'Ah, isn't it nice to be home again?' Davide remarked cheerfully as we entered.

But I couldn't follow his words as everything seemed to be spinning. Next, I felt Davide's hands embrace me with one quick move, preventing me from falling.

'Oh, gods! Patricia, what's wrong?' Lucretia's frightened voice sounded distant to me, despite being by my side.

'Call the physician immediately!' Davide commanded.

'No!' I protested weakly. 'There's no need. The journey must have exhausted me.'

'I insist ... my goddess,' Davide whispered pleadingly.

I shook my head in reply. There was no need for exaggeration. I only needed rest; I could already feel the strength coming back to my body.

'If I feel unwell again, I'll call the physician myself.' I considered the discussion over and let Lucretia lead me to my chamber. Perhaps one of those miraculous baths with aromatic oils she prepared so well would do the trick. Davide didn't persist further, yet I could sense his unease. My independence had pushed him away, leaving him feeling unwanted and unneeded. I was making my own decisions, and he didn't have a say in it.

The very next day, I was ready to visit my parents' home. I was desperate for advice, and only my mother could help with what I sought. Exposing Maurizio's true nature to Davide was my only priority, but my mother's teachings in the past had shown that a second chance was sometimes all a person needs.

'Daughter!' My mother's arms spread open, waiting for me. I hugged her tighter than usual as I felt safe once again in my childhood home. She looked deeply into my eyes for a long, quiet moment and then sat me on the sofa, taking the place next to me. 'You carry great happiness and responsibility.'

I frowned in confusion. 'What do you mean, mother?'

'You are with child,' she said lightly, as if stating the obvious – and, worse, as if it were good news.

I trembled as her words slowly spread through me. Was it possible I was with child? More precisely – was it so surprising? After all, I was in a sacred union with a man. It was more or less inevitable. But was I prepared for a child? For motherhood? No. There was no room for joy. To me, this only meant one thing – the bond between Davide and I would grow stronger, becoming unbreakable. And the love I so desperately looked for, the other half of my soul and heart, would be more and more like a mirage, an illusion that would fade away with each day my belly grew.

Reality hit me, sharp and sudden; although I'd agreed to this fate, I'd still had hope that somehow I might find my happy ending. Now, however, it became painfully clear that I would have to wait for the gods to grant me what I truly desired – if they ever intended to grant it at all.

In the heavy silence, my face betrayed every thought, and every emotion I felt. I didn't even ask my mother if she was certain – I believed her.

'You are a beam of light, Patricia. Never let yourself burn out. Always carry faith and hope within – never let them leave you,' my mother said gently as she brushed away my tears. She had read me like an open book.

My disappointment turned to grief, and then to a painful anger.

'Is it not enough to promise myself to a man I do not love? Must I have a child with him too? What hope can I have when I feel trapped?' I didn't try to keep my bitter words from her.

'A child is always a blessing, Patricia. If this is one of life's challenges, then let me share a secret: the gods send us only those trials we are strong enough to overcome. And life often proves to us how little we know about ourselves. But most importantly, the gods see all, and they act with justice when the time is right. Patience is the key.'

My visit ended far too quickly; no amount of time spent in my family home would ever feel like enough. But I had to return to Davide. I wouldn't be bringing him news about Maurizio today, but I would still surprise him with what I had to say.

As I arrived back at the estate, I headed straight to Davide's office. I had the unpleasant surprise of finding Maurizio there as well. The counsellor's expression at my appearance was nothing but disparaging.

'Excuse me for the intrusion, but I need to speak with my husband privately,' I said, keeping my expression neutral to avoid revealing the reason for my request.

'Of course,' Davide replied without hesitation, motioning for Maurizio to leave.

But Maurizio wouldn't be dismissed so easily, and as I expected, he attempted to stall. 'With all respect, dear Prefect, perhaps we ought to give a little more attention to the very important issue we were discussing?'

'It will wait until tomorrow,' Davide said firmly, demonstrating that his decision was not up for discussion.

The counsellor bowed and left the room with the slimiest courtesy of a smile – I wondered how the Prefect couldn't see it.

As soon as the doors closed, Davide approached me, taking my hands in his.

'Is everything all right?'

I imagined he was still worried about my health after nearly fainting the previous day.

'What I have to share will bring you only joy.' I forced my lips to stretch, resembling a smile. 'I am with child.'

The excitement that replaced the worry on his face was more than I expected. He lifted me into his arms, and the joyous laugh that filled the room seemed to come from the depths of his soul. His pure-hearted joy was almost enough to make me happy too. I smiled, now somewhat easier.

'This is the second time you've made me the happiest man in the world.'

Everything was about to change. I already knew that once a woman becomes a mother, her child becomes her world. Would I still be able to find room in my heart for the soulmate I had longed for, or would my child consume all my love, and I would no longer dream of him? Only time would tell.

*

Naively, I expected the changes in my body to happen instantly, but many sunrises and sunsets passed before that actually happened. I had plenty of time on my hands, plenty of opportunities to observe Maurizio and find out if he was up to something.

One evening, Davide entered our chambers with a smile. He settled next to me on the bed, kissed me tenderly, and rested his hands on my rounded belly. We sat in silence for a moment. I slid my hands over his shoulders and began to massage him gently. He closed his eyes, enjoying the peaceful moment. I could tell how much he cherished my presence.

'You are an incredible woman, and I consider myself blessed to have you.' His words startled me, not because I doubted his feelings but because I had never fully believed love could be so bizarre. 'From the moment I saw you, I knew I was irreversibly in love with you. But there was something else ... something deeper. I felt I could trust you.' He smiled, more to himself than to me. 'Trust is a luxury I can rarely afford. I was right to trust you, even when Maurizio urged me to think otherwise.'

At the mention of Maurizio's name, I shivered. He hadn't only dared to speak against me but had also not attempted to set things right and prove me wrong about him – there were no second chances available to give. My disappointment, however, was mixed with a dose of fear; I'd realised that Maurizio was a dangerous man, and my attempt to confront him might lead to failure. Sometimes, malice is too powerful to be defeated.

'He and I don't always share the same opinion, and our disagreements are sometimes large, but I don't understand what he holds against you,' Davide continued thinking out loud. His words invited a response, and I knew I had to be persuasive.

'Trust isn't freely given – it's built.' I spoke with a steady voice. 'I'm honoured to have earned yours. I want to be more than just your wife – I want to be your confidant, your partner and ... your counsellor. Together, we can accomplish so much more.'

My speech carried more intention than what Davide could have expected. Until that moment, I had shown him little emotion, but I meant every word. I believed we could be strong together if only he continued to be a better man than the one defined by his title.

Davide turned to meet my gaze. His eyes softened. It was easy to see his love for me, but his warmth couldn't reach my heart. It remained cold for him, as it was likely to remain.

'You are everything to me – you and our child.' He leaned down to kiss my belly, then returned to my lips.

*

Determined to expose Maurizio now more than ever, I instructed Lucretia to gather all possible information about him beyond his public affairs. I wasn't sure how useful it would be, but knowledge was power.

A few days later, Lucretia already had news for me, which was far faster than I'd been expecting. This suggested that Maurizio's reputation had earned him numerous enemies willing to speak against him. There was one way to find out. Away from curious eyes, in the garden, I listened intently to Lucretia's every word.

'It turns out that the traitor, like most men, loves to have fun.' She made a sour face at this last word. 'There's a difference in his preferences, though – he likes young men, too young for someone his age, if you ask me. He's known for his secretive and unpredictable behaviour and maintains powerful connections – I think they extend beyond the territory of the Prefect. Patricia, he's dangerous. Promise me you'll think your actions through!'

I nodded, though I knew the time for action had come. It was now or never.

'We'll talk again when you come back.' I needed her to run an errand for me, and she left in a hurry. What would I do without her?

I went back inside and walked down the corridor, lost in thought. I came out of my reverie at the sound of a voice coming from inside the library. Without a second thought, I went inside. As if summoned by my thoughts, there stood the very person who occupied them.

'Good day, Counsellor,' I greeted, not even bothering to feign pleasantness.

'Ah, Patricia, highly respected and so lovely.' A pretend smile spread across his face. His eyes narrowed into slits, making him look even more snake-like, and looked down at my belly. It made me shiver; I instinctively placed my hands protectively over it. There was something so horrifying about him, and Lucretia's news echoing in my mind didn't help. Everything in me screamed to turn around and go away. 'What a pleasant surprise to see you here,' he said, turning fully towards me and setting aside a parchment he'd been holding. Having me alone seemed to be amusing to him, as though it were an opportunity he'd been waiting for.

'Perhaps I was led by the same reason as you,' I replied, trying to keep my voice flat to hide the threat I was feeling.

'Ah, yes – knowledge, the greatest wealth of all,' he exclaimed, clapping his hands together with exaggerated delight. The sound startled me, and I struggled to suppress the urge to flinch. He noticed my reaction and satisfaction flashed in his eyes.

'Quite right. Unfortunately, our knowledge is limited, and our ignorance is boundless.'

'Perhaps, Patricia, perhaps,' he mused, pretending to consider my words, but from the gleam in his eyes, I didn't feel he actually shared my opinion. 'But those with a thirst for wealth often prosper, even more if they have a head for strategy, don't you think?' His question was rhetorical – Maurizio had no interest in my opinion.

'Depends on the perspective and the morals I suppose. I say the poor are not those who have nothing but those craving insensibly for more.'

'I'm afraid we'll have to agree to disagree there, dear.'

'Well, one sees only as much as one knows … dear,' I almost hissed.

He burst into a loud laugh. The mask of politeness fell away, revealing his true face: twisted and cruel.

'I've always enjoyed conversations with women,' he began – his tone condescending. 'Your eyes see only beauty, blind to the harsh reality of life. Reality is cruel! It's a brutal struggle where only the strongest survive. That's why we, the stronger sex, are given power – to rule – while you, the gentler sex, enjoy the comfort we provide.'

His face, distorted with delusional pride, looked like something of pure madness to me. People like him were dangerous, proving once again how sick ambition and corrupted power could rot the soul.

'We see the world differently; there's no argument,' I replied. 'The terror you're describing and finding yourself so comfortable living in must be avoided. We don't need chaos but a peaceful existence.' My effort was pointless – these words were meaningless to him. I might as well have been speaking to the books.

'Let me share a secret,' he said, leaning in close. I could feel his breath, reeking of wine. 'Only the weak one seeks order and allegiance – the strong one thrives in chaos.'

He was intoxicated by his own words, and I couldn't bear to spend another moment around him. 'I've taken enough of your time,' I said, pushing the conversation to an end.

'Not at all,' he replied with mock politeness, stepping back just slightly. 'It's always a pleasure. Perhaps we'll continue our discussion another time.'

I left the library without responding. My hands were trembling, and my heart was pounding as I escaped into the corridor. There was no room for regret now – what I was about to do felt unavoidable. The rest, I decided, would be left to the gods.

I sent word requesting the Prefect's presence and made my way to the garden – the only place where it felt safe to talk freely. Standing beneath the same tree where Davide and I had first spoken, I thought about life's strange sense of humour. Here I stood, awaiting him once again, just as I had unknowingly done on the night we met. Back then, I hadn't known he would become my husband. How many more of life's coincidences awaited me?

'I came as quickly as could,' Davide said.

'This is the only safe place to talk without fear of being overheard,' I said, watching his face twisting in confusion. 'The counsellor uses secret corridors to spy on nearly every room in this mansion. The most targeted places are your office and our chambers. I've seen it myself. I know you often have disagreements, and with such an advantage, he's far more dangerous than you realise. Davide, I have reason to suspect he's in conversation with nearby territories.'

Davide seemed unrecognisable to me. His jaw clenched, and every muscle on his body tightened. I could see the wave of emotions pass over him – shock, anger and betrayal.

'I kept a rat by my side for so long.' His voice was shaking with rage. 'Enemies lurk on all sides – I can't trust anyone.'

'We have no friends or enemies,' I said gently in an attempt to calm him down, 'only teachers. He deceived us all. But don't let anger cloud your judgment. Your actions must be wise – if he's as connected as I believe him to be, we need to be careful in dealing with him.'

A bitter smile crossed his face. 'Teachers, you say? Perhaps we can switch for once, and I can teach him a lesson.'

I reached for his hand, desperate to prevent another act of violence. 'Davide, please, don't make decisions in anger. It will only lead to regret.'

His hand rested briefly on my belly, but the determination in his eyes was unshaken.

'I'll fix the mistake I've tolerated for too long – for all our sakes,' he said, kissing me gently. His face softened for a moment before he turned and walked away, leaving me in fear. I wouldn't be able to live with myself if his actions led to bloodshed. How then would Davide be different from Maurizio?

*

I had expected news – any news. Surely, if something had happened with the counsellor, I would have heard by now, but days passed with Davide being silent about it, and I didn't want to press him. Perhaps he had listened to me after all and worked to resolve the situation without violence, setting aside his anger. The thought lit a flicker of pride in me, a victory worth cherishing.

One day, lost in thought, I took the wrong corridor on my way back to my chambers. Realising my mistake, I turned back with a smile, but my detour had brought me close enough to the library that I thought I'd quickly check in.

My eyes scanned the room as I stood before the wall where the secret door should have been, but the crescent moon from before was gone, the edges of the entrance that

I knew to be there were gone. I brushed my fingers along the shelf, but I found nothing. Stepping back, I looked over the entirety of the wall. It was different – it looked renewed. I couldn't quite piece together what this meant, but my body seemed to suspect something; I felt a sour feeling squirm into my stomach, and my hands already shook as I left to find Davide.

When I finally stood before his desk and I saw him sitting there, his face somehow harder than it had been, my mind joined my quivering body in its realisation.

'Where is he?' I finally managed to ask, though my voice was weak and low. Davide didn't flinch; he only tightened his jaw, and his eyes sharpened. *Murderer* – the word echoed in my mind. He was nothing I had hoped for; I understood this now.

He didn't speak, but it wasn't necessary – he'd told me everything. Suddenly my body felt unusually heavy, my feet didn't feel like they could support me anymore, my heart raced. I needed air; I began searching for it desperately, trying to get a big enough breath, but I couldn't seem to. A black fog began to descend around me. I wasn't scared. On the contrary, it was so comfortable I didn't try to fight it. I lent back into its arms, ominously embracing me. The last thing I felt were two strong hands, and then everything was lost in the darkness.

It felt good to float in nothingness, without worries, sadness, and, unfortunately, without happiness, but when there is no feeling, maybe happiness is irrelevant. Where was I? Perhaps this was the end? *I never found love*, I remembered. It didn't matter anymore; I didn't want to think about what I'd lost or had never gotten. I wanted to stay here forever, where there was peace.

Soon after, heat and light began to surround me.

'Patricia! Please come back!' This voice belonged to someone I didn't want to listen to. Davide pleaded with so much pain that my first reaction was to feel sorry that he was suffering, but even so, it wasn't enough for me to want to come back. But it was unavoidable – my eyelids slowly opened.

'I think she's waking up.' I heard Lucretia's voice, full of hope.

Slowly, the images before me became clear. Davide and my loyal friend were standing over me, and the anxiety on their faces was slowly replaced with relief.

'Can I speak with you about your wife?' someone said whom I couldn't see. A physician maybe.

Davide separated from me with reluctance, but that was exactly what I needed – a few minutes alone with Lucretia.

'You scared us! The Prefect was not himself—' she couldn't finish, interrupted by my weak voice, pressed by the little time we had.

'Do you know what happened to the Counsellor?' Something in my eyes was telling her I would not accept silence for an answer.

'On my responsibility, I refuse to speak …' As she said this, her posture was already crumbling under my gaze. 'Understand me, I wouldn't forgive myself if something happened to you again, if the news upset you so much that your condition got worse – think about the child!'

Of course, she was right, and I knew it, but I had to know what the man I was sharing my life with was capable of. Sooner or later, I would learn. The door opened and the Prefect returned with a smile. Lucretia saw a convenient moment to break away from our little conversation and walked away to bring me water.

'Such a relief it is to see your eyes. I could not bear to lose you, both of you!' He sat next to me and laid a hand on my belly.

Days after the incident, I could sense guilt in Davide, though he tried in vain to hide it. As for Lucretia, she was avoiding my eyes, worried I might press her further, but I had no intention of doing that – neither with her nor my husband. I decided to rely on one of my mother's precious lessons: patience always bears fruit in its time.

One evening just like any other, I was preparing for sleep. As my belly grew, so did my fatigue, and I often found comfort in my bed. I fell asleep instantly, and finally, it came to me – another, long-anticipated, dream.
I found myself in a room, my hands pressed on a desk for support. Beside me lay a blank parchment and a vial of ink. I was in a hurry. There was no time; the sense of urgency was growing with each passing second. I began to write.
My sun, my joy, my life, my Beatricia!

A soft, loving voice spoke to me in an effort to comfort me. Yet, as before, I couldn't see his face. I wanted to turn and see him, but the vision blurred, fading away like an illusion.
I opened my eyes abruptly, waking from the dream with my heart pounding wildly.
'Beatricia!' My anxious voice, almost a sob, broke the silence of the night.
Davide stirred beside me, pulling me into his arms.
'My love, what's wrong? Who is Beatricia?'
'Our daughter,' I whispered, just as confused as he was.

The pregnancy had changed me. I knew this was only the beginning; the true change would come with the first cry of my child. I rarely thought of *him* – the other half of my soul, wandering somewhere in this land, searching for me as I searched for him. Somehow, our paths remained uncrossed, and I began to doubt his existence at all.

The last dream, gifted by the gods, had not only given me my child's name but had also included *him*. I couldn't understand why, and truthfully, I wasn't sure I cared anymore. It was tempting to give in to pessimism, but that would be a mistake. My mother would say, *'Faith and hope should be your guides'*, but I was bitter.

Now, I would have h*is* substitute – someone who would never reject my love but would accept it unconditionally. Two little open arms would seek me out for comfort, and that would be my greatest joy.

*

The day when my life found its meaning and my soul was illuminated with light.

I could only feel one thing – a great pain. My feet gave out beneath me, and my knees hit the ground hard, but that didn't hurt, nor my hands scratching themselves along the walls as I slid. The agonising pain I was experiencing at that moment was dominating my senses. A groan escaped my lips … I was drowning in pain. I couldn't bear it. I couldn't cope with it.

Two hands lifted me up and moved me to the bed. Lucretia ran in and out, carrying water and towels. Several women were circling around me. I breathed. I was surrounded by people, but I was alone in this challenge – the sacred act of bringing life into this world.

A cry made everyone hold their breath. It was not mine but the tiny voice of a little defenceless being starting on life's long journey. A soul in a new body, ready for new adventures and lessons.

We were connected in a way only a mother and child could be. And I knew in that moment I needed nothing and no one but her.

Beatricia.

*

Life went on, or rather, a new life began for me. My pride and joy were incomparable. Caring for little Beatricia consumed me. Her every smile lifted me to the heavens; her every cry shattered me to pieces. She was my teacher, proving there was always more to learn. While I guided her through the world, helping her build habits and character, she was reshaping me. The ego I hadn't realised I had was completely erased, replaced by one focus: Beatricia. I loved watching her sleep, thinking about how she had taught me the true meaning of love. My mother's words once again echoed in my mind: *'We often think we're ready, until we realise we aren't at all!'*

*

One afternoon as Lucretia was bringing me tea, for the first time in months, I felt a rush of curiosity about the fate of the Counsellor. It had been so long that everyone else seemed to have forgotten, but not me.

'Lucretia, I need you to tell me what you know about Maurizio.'

She was completely unprepared for such a request, and for a moment she looked at me, confused and silent. But despite the inner conflict she faced, she seemed to resolve that it was time to reveal the truth.

'It's terrible,' she whispered. 'The Prefect was furious. Maurizio was summoned to the library, given a chance to confess and explain. But he denied everything – and even accused you of corrupting the Prefect's mind. This was his last mistake. Maurizio was injured and thrown into the tunnel. All exits and gaps were sealed, and finally the entrance itself. The Prefect had forbidden anyone to speak of it … but I have my ways to learn what I need.'

I listened without flinching. Barbaric violence, a vicious circle. Would it ever end? Even animals kill under natural laws to survive. Humans, however, make choices. We are nothing like animals – *choosing* violence is what turns us into beasts.

I realised my expectations of the Prefect had been too high. He was only a human, but I couldn't bear the weight of his choices. I could guide him to the right path, but he had to walk it himself. Davide showed no remorse. He was used to blood on his hands.

The truth about the Counsellor's fate had pushed me away from my husband; the fragile bridge we'd managed to build threatened to collapse. Yet, paradoxically, the more distant I grew, the more Davide leaned on me. Something genuine did still bind us together – our daughter. Davide adored her, calling her 'a little goddess, just like her mother'. She and I were his weakness – this is to say, we were what brought out his humanity. It didn't take long, however, until I came across the true shape of his love.

A feast. Another one, without any purpose but mere entertainment. In a small room, there he was, Davide, along with a nameless woman – a dancer perhaps, or a maid, maybe even a guest. She was giving him something I never could: passion.

'Get out!' Davide's rough voice commanded the woman when my unexpected appearance interrupted them.

She quickly covered herself and hid just outside the doors, where the music still amused the attendees. Davide stood guilty before me. But I knew it wasn't the act itself that unsettled him – it was the fact that it was no longer a secret to me. It was surprising to me, but also easy to believe. I remained silent. What I had just seen had no power over me. I didn't struggle to wipe the image out of my mind. There was no trace of jealousy. Instead, the realisation screamed in my head: *freedom*. For too long, I had been weighed down by the guilt of his love for me, knowing I could never return it. But now I knew that if I ever met the man from my dreams, I would be ready to embrace love fully.

'Say something.' Davide's voice broke, desperate. 'Your silence kills me ... is screaming without words my punishment.' He stood up and approached me with the look of a man ready to give everything. 'Show something ... Get angry, shout, just so I can see there's some feeling for me inside you.'

He looked almost pitiful in his despair, but I couldn't offer him the redemption he wanted.

'Silence doesn't mean there's nothing to say,' I replied calmly. 'It only means you're not ready to hear it.'

'Don't spare me,' he pleaded. 'Whatever you say, I deserve it. Just ... give me your attention.' I thought I could see tears in his eyes, but they might have been a product of the wine.

'They say the gods watch us from the heavens, judging us based on our deeds, but I believe they look from within, seeing through our desires, our hopes, and our sins.'

There was nothing more to add. I turned and left, leaving him with his thoughts. For the first time in years, I felt light, like a feather – as people were wont to say. I owed him no devotion. My respect for him as the father of our child was all that remained. Finally, I was free.

*

The mysterious dreams of the man didn't visit me as often as before. I felt forgotten by the gods, and my suspicion was confirmed when one of the first tragedies of my life came to pass – the death of my father, Emiliy.

I was completely unprepared, but it would be impossible to have been otherwise. Despite her own devastation and heartbreak, my mother again gathered her strength to be my support, to help me before helping herself. As a mother myself, I understood why she'd done this. She wisely reminded me that in life we are truly prepared for very few things, and death was not one of them. There was no proper time or proper comfort.

The pain was greater than anything I'd experienced, and the grief dragged me into a fog so dense I could feel nothing but tears on my face. Days blurred into darkness and a feeling of emptiness.

On the third day, my salvation arrived – a small, frightened face peeked through the opened doors of my chambers. Beatricia was the breath of air I needed to get out of the dark waters of oblivion.

Life and Death walk hand in hand as two sisters. To live fully, I realised I must embrace both. They are neither the beginning nor the end but part of something eternal. I would see my father again – of that, I was certain. Once connected, the gods ensure we meet again beyond this life.

*

The day my heart beat again – the day I began to truly live.

It was a beautiful day. The sun's rays caressed my skin warmly as I stood on the balcony watching birds flit about the garden. They knew no boundaries, landing on branches before flying away into the open sky again. *What did freedom feel like?* I smiled at myself for asking questions that had no answers.

My thoughts were flying as high as those birds despite having no wings of my own to spread – they had been cut off long ago. My place was here, grounded, bound to a man who had disappointed me, for even though I'd been freed from my guilt of not loving him, a woman couldn't simply leave – I knew this. And now my dear father had left this treacherous world to join the gods. My longing to find love had been slowly dying.

I had become like a stone sculpture – pierced by the goddess Juno, cursed not to feel the love I so longed for until I met my soulmate. Days and years had passed; I was thirty-three now, with no spark of hope remaining.

Yet I could not deny the blessings in my life – my mother, Lucretia, and most of all my daughter, a beautiful flower who bore little resemblance to her father and me. She was uniquely herself, and had the power to make me smile and to fill me with pride.

I closed my eyes, breathing the aroma that danced on the air, of life blossoming after winter. I ran my fingers over the pendant I'd carried for so many years, feeling the familiar engraving of the letter on it. For so long it had held a quiet presence against my skin. I never questioned why I clung to it so dearly.

Just as I was about to head inside, the pendant slipped from my fingers, and for the first time in all the years I'd had it, the chain gave way and it fell to the ground, sliding back to where I'd been standing. I walked over and bent to pick it up just as a melody came from the street below:

I look at you with eyes in love; they see not your body but your soul ... When I'm near you, it's easy to imagine our child, to see our hands, grown old, yet still fiercely entangled by the power of love. If you are not near me, I see only darkness.

The voice, copper-toned and melodic, reached me from afar. It belonged to a young man. The melody was intoxicating for me. It caught me off guard. My entire being vibrated, and for the first time, I knew what it was like to feel truly afraid – I was afraid the voice would stop and I would be left without it. What was happening to me? I had to see the man behind the voice. Just like in my dreams, for good or bad, I had to find him.

I ran down the corridor to the garden. I would follow the music to its source. The fewer witnesses, the better, so I hoped luck would be on my side.

'Patricia, I just—' I passed by Lucretia, who was obviously looking for me. I left her speechless, watching after me as I sped away, but I quickly calculated that I would need her help, so I stopped abruptly and turned back.

'I want you to accompany me for a walk,' I said, too flustered to hide my excitement and in too much of a hurry to address the look of confusion spread across her face.

'The Prefect sent me to find you. He's in the garden with some of the senators and insists you join them immediately.'

I wasn't surprised. Davide was a constant obstacle in my life. But not this time!

'Well, so be it,' I replied.

Lucretia looked puzzled. She must have expected me to refuse, but I followed her quietly. Under a spacious shed, comfortably equipped with soft chairs around a table full of drinks and food, Davide's loud laughter was spreading across the garden. The reason for the meeting was already blurred by the wine, and their talk was far from that of political issues. Everybody seemed amused, and as I approached, they stood up to greet me. Despite the years, my glory as the most beautiful woman in the city had not diminished, and I could feel the lustful looks sweeping over me, but it wasn't worth the contempt.

'My goddess!' Davide exclaimed, reaching forward with his open hands in expectation.

As usual, he showed love, unlike me. I ignored his gesture. Instead, I stepped closer to whisper in his ear: 'There's a musician outside – more talented than anyone. I want to see him.'

He looked at me, confused, amused by the wine, upset for me not having returned the gesture of affection, and astonished by the unexpected request.

'There is nothing I cannot give you,' he finally said only for me to hear, but the intimacy carried in those words had no interest to me, so I remained silent, waiting.

'Well, gentlemen,' he announced with a note of disappointment only I could detect, 'it seems my wife has discovered a musician outside these walls who has impressed her – something, I assure you, does not happen often.'

The men murmured in interest as Davide ordered the guards to find the musician. He then poured me a glass of wine in the hope that we would enjoy a shared moment together, but I refused – my trembling hands would betray me. All the patience I had learned over the past years was now of no use to me. To distract myself, I tried to imagine the face of the stranger with a beautiful voice; perhaps at that moment, he was frightened by the sudden appearance of guards who, without explanation, would drag him from wherever he was and whatever he was doing.

The conversation resumed, the focus shifted away from me, and the time dragged more than I could possibly force myself to wait. Had the guards found him?

Finally, I heard footsteps behind me. I didn't turn immediately, though every fibre of my being urged me to. Instead, I looked at Lucretia, and her eyes sparked with curiosity. The guards were not alone – a stranger had come with them. Everyone fell silent as Davide began to speak.

'Here he is, the most talented among them all!' Davide's tone was mocking, and everyone laughed. His behaviour irritated me – unnecessary and petty, driven no doubt by the wine and his frustration over my coldness.

For a moment, all eyes were on the guest. Something in that brief moment of not knowing his face felt special to me.

'Forgive me, Prefect,' the quiet voice of the musician spoke out. 'I didn't mean to disturb your peace with my music.'

The sound of his voice struck me. It was something familiar yet impossible for me to place.

'You did nothing wrong, boy,' Davide replied, this time a touch more sincere. 'On the contrary, your talent was appreciated by my wife – not an insignificant accomplishment.' He turned to me with a smirk. 'My dear, won't you give him your attention, since you are the reason for his presence among us?'

I felt fear, not of the man but of what his presence meant. A change was coming, one that I sensed would impact me forever. Finally, I turned to face him. At first, I seemed unable to fix my gaze on him. Then I saw him – kneeling, trembling like a leaf, surrounded by guards. His head was bowed, leaving his face in shadow. Frustrated for not being able to see him clearly, I stepped closer, closer than what would have been considered appropriate, but I dared anyone to challenge me in that moment.

'Stand up,' I said, more as a request than a command.

Hesitantly, he got his feet below him and pushed himself to full height. At last, he stood before me. He was tall and well-built, yet his face remained a mystery as he'd kept his head bowed. I wanted to see his eyes. Reading someone had never been a problem for me, until this moment, and I was frustrated.

'Lift your head.' The words slipped out sharper than intended.

'Boy, don't be afraid. You are here as a guest. Don't anger my wife anymore – this is something even I avoid if I can,' he shouted, making his guests laugh even louder. I didn't pay attention to them; they were like shadows, a distant echo that didn't interest me.

The musician's eyes finally met mine; warm and brown, they embraced me.

Later, Lucretia would tell me the story of how quickly everything had happened. *'In the space of a breath,'* she'd said. Through the years, long after that, I would go back to this memory, reminding myself with delight of the incredible feeling of that brief but significant moment in my life.

The guards were ready to strike him down as I had fallen unconscious. No words would be suitable enough to describe what had happened to me – I leave that challenge to any poet brave enough to take it on. As the musician's eyes wrapped me in warmth and calm, for the first time in my life, I felt at peace with myself. But most importantly, I recognised him – it was *him*. Suddenly, I could see beyond that moment, visions of us, passing fast before my eyes – he and I together in every life.

Different faces, different times, but the same souls, meeting each other again and again. The forgotten memories had overwhelmed my stunned senses. My human body was incapable of accepting this knowledge, and it failed, weak under the power of awareness.

I sank back into the darkness, alone. I was well and familiar with this place. The difference was that now I didn't want to stay; I wanted to go back to the light, where I knew I was going to see him!

The darkness, however, did bring its own lucidity: Life was like a game; we lived surrounded by people we didn't remember. We search and meet, starting from the beginning a thousand times. People were limited creatures, doomed to eternal wandering, with questions that had obvious answers we were too blind to see. For good or for bad, this was our karma. We think we're at the top of the pyramid, but we actually don't know anything about ourselves or our abilities. We were capable of so much!

I opened my eyes and found myself in the familiarity of my chambers. Feverishly, I started looking for the musician, but instead, I met Lucretia's concerned eyes. She sighed in relief and her lips curved into a faint smile.

'Where is he?' I asked, attempting to stand up too quickly.

'Patricia! Are you trying to frighten us even more? You need to rest.' She gently pressed me back onto the bed, but I pushed her hand away.

'Where is he?' I repeated.

'The physician said today is one of the warmest days of the year,' she began, ignoring my question. 'It's natural for someone to faint in this heat, but we were still worried—'

'Where is he!' I grabbed her roughly, her servant's uniform clutched in my fists. Her horrified expression told me I must have looked mad, but I didn't care. I had to know.

'In his office,' she answered quickly.

'The Prefect doesn't matter to me. The musician. Where is he?'

'Since when does an unknown man matter to you?' she asked incredulously and gave me a final quick look, no doubt evaluating my condition. She reached for a cold cloth and went to put it on my forehead, but I stopped her, now calmer, my hand steady. 'I cannot say for sure because they took him away,' she continued, 'and we were all busy taking care of you ... But I heard – by the Prefect's order – that he was sent to another estate until his guilt or innocence could be determined.'

I practically jumped out of bed, unusual for a person who had just regained consciousness. As I rushed to Davide's office, I heard Lucretia calling after me, but I didn't slow.

Despite my frantic desire, my *need* to see him, my mind was calm, sharp, but I had to be careful – I'd fainted and was now rushing about the mansion in perfect health. It was atypical to say the least, and I couldn't afford to draw suspicion, not with so much at stake. I needed privacy, time alone with the musician, and discretion was key.

Before entering Davide's office, I took a moment to steady myself. As I finally entered, I found Davide with a maid in his lap. It was nothing new at this point – my disappointment and disgust towards him had long since faded into indifference. Perhaps, at another time, I might have questioned how he interpreted the word 'respect' –

the fact he went after other women when he thought me unconscious spoke a lot of his character. But none of that mattered now. It would never matter again as the gods had finally revealed my path.

'Out!' he yelled at the girl – her cheeks flushed as she scurried away. 'My goddess! What a comfort and joy it is to see you on your feet again, illuminating my day with your presence.' He extended a hand, inviting me closer, but I barely even glanced at his gesture of affection.

'I didn't mean to interrupt,' I replied, 'but I wanted to inform you that I'm feeling better.' I planned to provoke his guilty conscience, knowing it meant he'd grant any wish of mine. My little trick worked instantly.

'Is there anything I can do to make you happier, darling?'

'I was wondering about the musician,' I said lightly, as though the question were an afterthought.

'Ah, him.' Davide's expression darkened slightly. 'Forgive me, but you must admit the circumstances didn't favour him. I had him sent to the seaside estate, far from here. If he was indeed the cause of your condition, I wanted to ensure he was not a threat. But I've realised I may have acted too hastily. No harm will be done to the young man. In fact,' he added, 'he seemed horrified himself when you fainted.'

'Very well,' I said, still trying to sound casual. 'Then I suppose we'll have an occasion to visit my favourite estate.'

Davide studied my face for a moment before nodding. 'Of course. We haven't been there in ages. If the musician proves talented enough, he can entertain us with his music. It's a splendid idea,' he said, now enthused by his plan.

I nodded and turned to leave, pausing briefly at the door. 'Let me know when we're leaving.'

I didn't eat or sleep in the days that followed; I was consumed by questions and anticipation. But what did I hope for? Even if this stranger shared my feelings, what could come of it? Escape together? A shameless affair in plain sight of the Prefect? I had no freedom to follow my heart. I never had. Perhaps the musician had come into my life too late. Another time, another life, perhaps, but not now.

Despite everything, I played my part well. Davide suspected nothing, but Lucretia saw through me – she always did. She had been faithful not out of duty but a sister's love for me, a bond deeper than obligation. I could never keep secrets from her – especially not now, when I needed her more than ever.

The long-awaited news came days later: we were to leave for the seaside mansion the following day. The thrill of the unknown was electrifying; my heart would randomly begin racing with a mix of fear and excitement. I had asked Beatricia to stay with my mother. The thought of leaving her behind pained me – this was to be our first time apart – but I knew it would be best to shield her from whatever was to come. It was the only way.

I found her in the garden. This wasn't a big surprise to me; just like her mother, and admittedly her father as well, she loved being around nature, but there seemed to be more of me in her than of Davide. I could see a bright future on the horizon for her. Soon, I would tell her the family secret and pass on our knowledge, but for now, my path was elsewhere.

I approached my daughter and stroked her golden hair. The sun gave it a warm, coppery glow.

She turned to me with a smile.

'I knew I'd find you here,' I said, sitting beside her on the bench.

'And I knew you'd come here.' Her response made me smile.

'I have something to tell you.'

'I wanted to talk to you too.' Her expression seemed distant, her gaze wandering somewhere ahead.

'Really? Then you start.'

'No, I'm sure yours is more important,' she insisted with a small shake of her head.

'Fine.' I took a deep breath. 'I'd like you to accompany your grandmother for a while.'

'For how long?' she asked immediately, without a trace of surprise or confusion.

'I don't know yet.' I admitted after a pause. The truth was that my future was uncertain, but I was struck by my daughter's odd reaction; it was restrained, almost detached. 'There's no reason to be sad if that's what you're feeling,' I added quickly, trying to reassure her. 'We will return soon.'

'Patricia,' Lucretia's voice called out from the distance. It must have been important.

I stood, promising to finish the conversation with my daughter later, but just as I turned to leave, her quiet words stopped me.

'I have a bad feeling.' The words were said more to herself and the air than to me.

I laid a hand on her shoulder, struggling to mask the worry I knew must be showing on my face.

'That was what I wanted to tell you,' she added with eyes still fixed far ahead.

'Patricia,' Lucretia called again with urgency.

It was one of those moments when there was so much to say and no room to say it.

'I promise nothing bad will happen,' I said, forcing a smile. 'Trust me.' Even as the words left my lips, I knew my smile didn't reach my eyes.

The next day, everything was ready for our journey. I kissed Beatricia goodbye and promised to return soon, but in my heart, I wondered if this was a promise I'd be able to keep.

I tried to push away the dark thoughts and focus on the excitement of what lay ahead. The feeling of meeting with the mysterious man was beyond comparison – I felt I could walk the entire distance to the sea. I needed no horses or escort to delay me. I wanted to fly – to my freedom, to the place where my heart was calling me.

*

I burned with anticipation to see the musician, but I knew that any sign of eagerness could raise suspicion. If I wanted the privacy I so desperately needed, I had to be patient, pretending that seeing him couldn't possibly be a priority for me. I only knew that the musician was being kept somewhere within the estate, locked away – but exactly where, I had yet to discover. It was in everyone's best interest if I played like nothing had changed.

I caught Lucretia's hand, just as we used to do when we were young girls, and we walked together down the path to the shore. With every step, I breathed in the salty air, letting it spread through every part of my being. The waves whispered their song as they dissolved into the sand, and the birds flew gracefully over in the azure expanse, their cries echoing in harmony with the rhythm of the sea. I wanted to stay there forever, but while this isolated estate suited me, it was utterly unfit for the Prefect. Our differences were vast, just like the waters I now looked over.

A childish joy filled me as the waves – soft and gentle – kissed my feet. The winds of change whispered to me that something was about to happen in my life, and though the unknown usually brought fear, this time I felt ready for whatever might come my way. I was incredibly blessed to have Lucretia by my side, sharing my happiness and holding me steady when life tried to crush me. Beatricia, too, gave me strength simply by existing – she was my motivation to keep moving forward. And now, the thrill of passion and true romance had entered my life, a new force I was eager to explore.

Davide, of course, was blind to the truth, but his inner voice was no doubt whispering something to him. I knew he felt me slipping away – that I had never belonged to him. Unfortunately he was too sunken into the material world to actually heed these signs, forgetting his roots. I had tried to guide him, to awaken him to his own divine origins. I had shown him kindness and compassion, but it wasn't easy to break the shell of a stiffened heart. After years of effort, I was exhausted. Truth and knowledge could often make a person lonely, and I had lived as an isolated soul for so long. But that time was over.

Davide had arranged a celebration for our arrival. I had no interest in the food or anything around me; my thoughts were consumed by the guest of honour – the musician.

'Bring him in,' the Prefect commanded.

The heavy doors swung open and he entered, pale faced with wide, frightened eyes. Pushed forwards by the guards, our guest clutched his musical instrument tightly, his eyes darting from face to face until they met mine.

The world around us fell away. His gaze pierced right through me. My senses stretched taut like the strings he held clutched in his hand, yearning for his touch. I wanted to go to him instantly, but my mind fought against the impulse, keeping me in place.

Then Davide's voice shattered the moment.

'Well, young man,' he said in a tone laced with irony, 'I hope you've enjoyed my hospitality. Now it's my turn to enjoy your music ... I hope.'

The room fell silent. All eyes were on the musician, and the attention and expectation were clearly too much for him. His hands trembled as he attempted to play, and the melody barely resembled the haunting tune I had clung to in my memory.

Davide interrupted the awkward scene with a cruel laugh. 'My goddess,' he said, turning to me, 'has this musician impressed you? He's not even fit to play on the streets!'

The room erupted in laughter.

'Perhaps the guards have brought us the wrong man,' he added mockingly.

'Do you doubt my judgment?' I said coldly. Davide's laughter ceased, and his expression darkened. 'Anyone would be intimidated in the presence of the Prefect himself. Let's give him another chance.'

Davide studied me, searching for answers he would never find. Then, with a shrug, he agreed. 'So be it.'

The room fell silent again as all eyes turned back to the musician, who in turn, closed his own eyes, inhaled deeply, and began to play.

The beauty of the melody that then filled the room was even more profound than I remembered. The music was enchanting, silencing even the most sceptical – Davide. A smile crept onto my face.

When the final tune faded, the room was still. All waited for Davide's reaction. After a moment, he clapped his hands with uncharacteristic excitement.

'Amazing!' he declared. 'I confess, I underestimated you. But that's in the past. It's decided – you'll play for me from now on. How do they call you?'

'Martel,' the musician answered, a little more confidently.

Davide nodded, pleased. 'Well, my dear,' he said, turning to me, 'wasn't this worth the wait? Tell me, are you pleased with my gift to you?'

'Your generosity knows no bounds,' I replied, 'but now that Martel is part of our household, perhaps we shouldn't keep him locked up.'

'Of course not. I'm not a tyrant,' Davide said with a laugh. 'He'll enjoy his freedom at the mansion where he can entertain us with his music.'

'I trust he was treated with care during his stay?'

'More than that actually,' Davide said, grinning. 'As soon as I knew he wasn't guilty of your sudden condition, I arranged for a dozen girls to see to his every need. I'm sure he'll never forget my generosity.' He was amused by the thought.

I watched Davide, repelled by his simple thinking. A surge of unfamiliar emotion swept over me, sharp and bitter – jealousy.

Later that evening, I made my way to Martel's room. The corridors were empty, and I moved silently, clinging to the walls at the slightest sound. My heart raced.

When I reached his door, I hesitated. My palms were sweaty, and my breath quickened. What awaited me on the other side could change everything.

Summoning my courage, I knocked softly.

The door opened almost immediately. Martel stood before me with an odd expression, an expression befitting the moment – a mixture of surprise and expectation. He stepped back, silently inviting me in. I entered and closed the door behind me. Our eyes locked in a silent moment. I had imagined this countless times, rehearsing what I might say. Yet now, faced with him, my thoughts scattered. But what of him? Did he feel the same? Our connection across lifetimes, our forgotten memories – had they been revealed to him as they had to me?

The questions were many, words insufficient, and the time scarce, yet his eyes held the answers I sought. Deep within, I knew the time had come for us to find and unite with each other, in this life, and I knew how we would do it. Fortunately, inspired by the tunnel in the library, I'd long ago gotten curious about the Prefect's other estates. Hidden escape routes seemed to be an old staple in the properties of the leadership, a detail Davide seemed unaware of, no doubt having been kept in the dark by Maurizio.

'At the end of the corridor, there's a statue in the corner. Behind it, low to the ground, there's a brick, lighter in colour than the others. Push it and a passage will appear before you. Inside, you'll find a lit torch – use it to light your path. It will lead you to the shore. I'll wait for you there,' I whispered.

'I'll be there,' he replied, his voice thick with emotion. His eyes never left mine.

I forced myself to leave, my body resisting every step as if defying my will. I could hardly recall a time when it took such a monumental effort to control my actions.

As I made my way back, I heard voices echoing down the corridor, approaching quickly. It was Davide, and several other people. Their voices were low, tense, as if discussing a grave matter. My body went rigid, but as they passed, I was surprised to find they didn't notice me. Davide, who rarely let anything escape his attention, didn't even glance in my direction.

Curiosity made me stop and turn, watching him retreat down the hall. My biggest concern was my secret, but whatever worried Davide, whatever trouble he had was surely significant – passing by me like I was invisible was more than unusual. A strange feeling of uneasiness overtook me, and my gut twisted unpleasantly. Was it a sign from the gods, or was I seeing omens where none existed? For once, I felt that whatever troubled Davide was no longer my battle to fight. I had my own path now.

I reached the statue with the hidden passage I had described to Martel. Ensuring the corridor was empty, I knelt and found the brick. I pushed it and the entrance opened itself. I lit two torches, placing one where Martel would find it, and vanished into the dim passage. The shadows played tricks on my mind, stirring memories of how Counsellor Maurizio was spying on us, but the passage was short, and soon, the cool night air greeted me as I emerged on the other side.

I walked across the sand, seeking a spot away from prying eyes. A large, smooth rock stood between the sea and the path to the estate. It was a perfect barrier. I settled on the far side of it and waited.

Not long after, I heard steps approaching, but I didn't look back. They stopped a short distance away, not quite approaching me. Was Martel unsure? Afraid? After a pause, the steps resumed and he came up beside me. He sat, not too close, but close enough.

I could hear my own heartbeat, and I wondered if Martel could hear it too. I didn't turn to greet him; instead, I continued to watch the sea, now a dark, polished marble under the night sky.

Just hours ago, etiquette and circumstances had kept us apart. Now, with only the stars as witnesses, he sat freely by my side. My hands ached to reach for his, to bridge the gap between us. The silence wasn't awkward but natural, like that held by dear friends.

'The day I saw you for the first time …' Martel's voice trailed off before he could finish.

'Yes,' I replied, knowing what he was trying to say.

'So strong …'

'It was.'

He turned to me, and I met his gaze. In that moment, every barrier between us dissolved. Fear, restraint, and hesitation melted away. A force greater than either of us drew our bodies together.

Our lips found each other with passion, tender and consuming. Every touch, every kiss was an explosion of emotion – a reunion of souls.

When our bodies rested, entwined on the sand, Martel looked to the stars while I studied his face. His beauty was undeniable, but it wasn't what had captivated me. My love was for the essence of him, that which felt so deeply familiar. A love like this could not be a crime or infidelity – we belonged to each other. I could devote myself to him without any shame.

Martel turned to me with eyes full of wonder. 'I feel as if I've known you, but I don't truly have you.'

'You never lose what truly belongs to you,' I assured him, my fingers brushing his hair. 'The gods brought us together, and they will continue to guide us. Have faith in them.'

He kissed our joined hands as he kept his eyes on mine.

I could have stayed there forever, lost in his presence, but time was not on our side. We stood up with reluctance and took the way back. The silence between us now carried weight, as if the night itself understood the fragile, dangerous nature of our bond. What we desired and what was allowed were worlds apart. Still, as we walked side by side, I longed to reach for his hand, to feel the warmth of his touch. But if anyone saw us …

Like thieves, we sneaked in the dark, hoping we went unnoticed, and that we would be able to preserve what we had. It all felt so strange. I was not a criminal; I was entitled to happiness, and I wanted the freedom to enjoy it.

The moon illuminated the last, quickly given kiss.

Later that same evening, as I prepared to rest, I reached for my pendant to place it in my jewellery box, as usual. But I felt the strange desire to look at it up close again. The engraving was so delicate and beautiful, but it was hard to get a clear look at it in the dim lighting. I concluded that it indeed looked like an initial, the letter M …

I jumped like I'd been stung. Was this a mere coincidence? How had I not realised this before? I had carried Martel's initial close to my heart – a sign showing me my path. The gods had once again been proven mighty, and I had doubted them for no reason.

That night was calm. For the first time in years, there were no strange dreams – I had no one to search for.

*

Standing before the mirror, I looked at my reflection with vanity. I arranged my hair in my favourite way, I tried different jewels, changing them with disapproval, as if I was preparing for an event, but there was nothing of the sort. The only reason was Martel.

The doors opened with a crash, startling me. Davide stood behind me in the mirror. His expression was wild, like someone who'd lost their mind.

'We're leaving, tomorrow!' he declared.

I turned slowly, meeting his eyes but remaining silent and calm, though panic gripped me.

'Why are you silent? Won't you say something?' he demanded, slamming his fist on a table, sending a bowl of fruit to the floor. But I didn't flinch. His face, twisted in frustration, suddenly softened and revealed despair. The man in front of me was ready to collapse. 'Don't you understand?' he said with a breaking voice. 'You always seem to know everything – I need you now more than ever!'

I opened my arms, inviting him into my embrace. He crossed the room with a few big steps and sank to his knees, burying his head in my lap like a child.

I caressed him while holding my breath in anticipation of the reason that led to this outburst.

'Terrible things are happening,' he murmured. 'Dangerous takeovers ... My position is at stake, but if I return to the capital, I can resist them. I'm strong. No one can defeat me.' His words felt more like self-reassurance than confidence.

My daughter's warning echoed in my memory. Even Beatricia had sensed the storm coming while I had been blinded by my personal happiness.

'Whatever happens, my place is not there, nor is Beatricia's. She must come here immediately,' my words sounded more like an order, although my voice was shaken by a sudden fear. My daughter's place was next to me, and at the same time, I couldn't leave Martel.

Davide sighed. 'Of course. Forgive me. You and Beatricia are my priority. Both of you must stay far from danger.' His voice softened. 'I've relied on you so heavily that I'd forgotten you're my wife, and it's my duty to protect you. I can't take you where even my own life is at risk.'

We remained locked in the moment for a while, his head in my lap as he looked for salvation, and I unable to offer what he needed. Though years had passed since our union, Davide still felt like a stranger to me. Exhausted by years of giving, I had nothing left to offer.

When Davide spoke again, his tone had steadied. 'I have to leave at dawn. More guards will come to ensure your safety and Beatricia's.'

I nodded gratefully and he stood up ready to leave his moment of weakness behind. Just as he reached the door, he paused.

'You know ... it feels like I'm saying goodbye,' he said. He shook his head as if to drive away a dark thought, and then he left, leaving me alone and scared.

Was this a sign from the gods? Why did joy and dread go hand in hand? What lesson awaited me now?

That night, I was restless, waiting for what felt like the inevitable. I wondered if Davide would come to me for comfort before his departure, and the thought filled me with disgust. It felt as if I would betray Martel, the man to whom I did not belong lawfully.

A sudden noise in the corridor broke my thoughts. I opened the door to see the guards struggling to carry someone. For a heart-stopping moment, I feared it was Martel, but I quickly realised that it wasn't. I went out of the room and ordered the guards to stop.

'What is this chaos at this time?' I demanded.

'The Prefect ordered us to escort him to his chambers. Forgive us for the noise,' said a young boy, visibly anxious as he supported the Prefect's weight.

It was clear that Davide had drunk himself into oblivion. I dismissed the guards with a wave of my hand and returned to my chambers. This wasn't typical of Davide, especially at such a critical time. It spoke of despair – a man already resigned to defeat.

I curled up on my bed and sank into my thoughts. Something was about to happen. All the signs were pointing towards this inevitable fact, but I still couldn't predict how bad it would be.

*

Days passed, each blending into the next as though time itself had paused. Martel and I talked, laughed and made love. I was now certain that I had known Martel across many lifetimes. I had seen different faces and had kissed different lips, but it was always the same soul, always him ... always us two. I didn't know why we were destined to find and lose each other over and over again, why we were fated to seek and suffer, to wander endlessly apart only to reunite. But one thing I knew for sure – the sweetest feeling was the moment of recognising each other once again. When every fibre of your being shouts *'It's him!'*, you simply feel it – a sixth sense.

Despite my endless happiness, Beatricia never left my thoughts. My worry for her grew with each passing day. Why wasn't she here yet?

I waited.

Time was ticking away in moments of happiness and moments of anxiety.

I waited.

*

It was late afternoon. Martel and I were relaxing on the balcony, enjoying the gentle breeze, a platter of fresh fruits and matured wine. I wore one of my favourite robes – an airy white garment trimmed with embroidered patterns along the edges. We spoke of freedom, of life, of everything and nothing.

Then, suddenly, Martel's words were blurred by a small commotion below us. I leaned over the balcony. Exhausted horses had just arrived. A loud crash startled me, and I realised the glass I'd been holding was now shattered on the balcony floor. The red wine stained my robe, looking like blood. A chill swept over me; someone's blood had been spilled. Someone had died.

Martel jumped to his feet and held my face to meet my eyes.

'Are you all right, my love? Are you hurt?' His voice trembled, but I had no time to reassure him.

The doors of my chambers opened loudly. Lucretia stumbled in, unable to catch her breath. Her wide, horrified eyes told me everything before she could speak. When she opened her mouth, only a mournful cry escaped, and my heart stopped.

'Speak, Lucretia! Speak, or we are all doomed!' Martel's begging voice broke the suffocating silence.

I couldn't move, couldn't breathe. My world was on the edge of collapse.

'Patricia ...' Lucretia finally managed between the sobs. 'He had no way to escape – they trapped him. The Prefect has been murdered ... the mansion overtaken. But we received news that Beatricia is hiding with your mother at your family home.'

My feet betrayed me, and I felt the sudden roughness on the floor against my knees. Martel's hands came to me, pulling me up from the dark sea in which I was sinking. Even if everything around me collapsed, I had to stay strong. A mother's heart knows no despair apart from the first cry of her child – it beats with resilience. I could not afford to be weak at this moment.

'Lucretia, order the horses to be prepared immediately! I'm riding to the capital.'

'Please, Patricia, be wise – if you go now and they catch you, they will kill you! You are the Prefect's wife.' Lucretia pleaded with me to see reason. 'Let me go instead, with one of the servants. I won't attract attention. We'll take hidden paths and reach your family house in no time. I'll bring them back safely – I promise!'

'I will call for a servant.' Martel didn't wait for my reply; he rushed through the door, leaving me no chance to argue as they both knew I would. My safety was their priority, but it wasn't mine. Still, this plan carried the least risk, and I had to admit that.

I hurried to the desk, grabbed a bit of parchment, and began writing:

My sun, my joy, my life, my Beatricia! We have lost
too much to suffer another tragedy. I beg you,
as soon as you receive this letter, prepare for an
immediate journey. No sleep or peace will come
to me until I can hold you again. You will
always be a part of me. I love you.
Your mother.

Folding the letter as best as I could with my trembling hands, I handed it to Lucretia. 'You must give this to my daughter,' I said. Even through my distress, I noticed that something was off with her.

'What are you not telling me?' I asked.

She hesitated, then sobbed. 'I don't think it would matter to you … but I think you should know this.'

'If it's a burden, release yourself from it now,' I encouraged.

After a heavy sigh, she began. 'The day the Prefect left, he waited for you … to say goodbye, I think. But you didn't come. He was angry, but I could tell it was only his pain speaking. He ordered me to call you, and I told him the truth, that you were asleep. He didn't believe me and pushed me aside to enter your chambers. He found you asleep ... so peaceful, so innocent. He watched you for a moment, and I saw something break in him. His anger melted, but sadness remained. He kissed you gently and left. It was the last time he saw you.' Her voice broke as she finished.

Last kiss, last goodbye ... as always, I wasn't a participant. It was never meant to be for him and me, and even though I'd always known this, guilt and sorrow pierced my chest. 'Thank you,' I whispered. 'You thought right – I needed to know that.'

I had experienced grief once before, and life brought me back to that trial. I reflected once again on if death really was an end or a beginning. I wanted to believe that, in another life, I might once again meet the people I had lost.

Footsteps interrupted my thoughts. Martel had returned.

'The horse is ready, Lucretia,' he said, and I noticed he didn't look directly at her. Martel, who had quickly become like family with Lucretia, now seemed willing to risk her life over mine. It was human nature, I supposed, to protect what we hold dear. The thought of anyone risking themselves for me felt unbearable, but I was outnumbered. Both Martel and Lucretia wanted to shield me out of unconditional love. Was I blessed, or destined to lose everything? Only time would tell.

I wiped away my tears, and the three of us went to the entrance of the house. A young boy, Francesco, waited there. He was the son of one of our most loyal helpers. Stretched like a string, proud to be assigned an important task, he seemed like a warrior on his first mission, eager to prove himself. He had kind eyes, a pure soul – innocent. He had a beautiful face, but he still held the rounded features of youth. He was no less than fifteen years old, just like my daughter.

Francesco helped Lucretia onto the horse and swiftly sat behind her.

'I'll see you soon!' she said with a trembling chin as tears streamed down her face. Then they tore away, flying down the path. Moments later, they were gone.

The dust was still hanging in the air, marking where they had just been. I stood motionless, unable to take my eyes off the fading trail. A heavy weight twisted painfully in my chest.

Martel urged me to return to the house, but I couldn't move. My eyes stayed fixed on where I'd last seen them, memorising the moment.

*

Everything happened so fast it didn't feel real, more like a dream, a very bad one. Martel's beautiful voice was deep, determined. His gentle face was somewhat different as well – serious, hard, fearless. His lips moved, saying something, but the words didn't reach me; I couldn't connect them into a logical sentence. Still, some of the words got through: 'run', 'I promise', 'fast', 'will be fine', 'run'. I followed him; he had finally stopped pulling me by force. If Martel wasn't there with me, I wouldn't be among the living.

It's in moments like these that one sees how strong and prepared one is. I was neither. When my feet surrendered and I collapsed under my burden of sorrow, when my consciousness gave up power over my body, when I just wanted to die and the chaos surrounded me – people running, crying for help – a strong hand stood me up and pulled me forward to salvation.

*

I awoke, disoriented, on the deck of a ship. What would have normally been a surprise didn't matter to me in the slightest.

I fell asleep and woke up countless times, each time wondering where I was. Eventually, I realised, and then I lost consciousness again. I could hear Martel's voice, talking to someone, maybe the captain or part of the crew, or maybe just someone like us, who had managed to save themselves.

Again, this did not matter to me – I couldn't bring myself to be curious, to care.

But what did matter to me then?

There was a memory swimming deep in the waters of me, circling low in the dark, a memory of what had just happened, what had brought us to be where we were now. I didn't want to bring up that little swimming memory, out of the water up into the light. I wanted to let it keep swimming down there in the depths of me. Each time I did begin to call it to the surface, a scream clawed its way up with it, but I'd stifle it before it escaped and release the memory to sink back down. I'd open my eyes and listen to the waves sloshing and slapping against the side of the ship, feeling the vessel sway this way and that, but as soon as I closed my eyes, the memory burned brighter, swam more frantically, splashing and flipping. The only thing I felt I could do was open my eyes again, sitting bolt upright, tears forming. I desperately wanted to free myself from this feeling.

And then I would feel him – his hands, gentle and firm, reminding me that he wouldn't allow me to fall apart. Martel would always be by my side, the man who appeared in my life to show me the meaning of happiness, to save my soul from wandering endlessly in search of love ... and now, to save me from destruction.

'I'm here,' he whispered. 'It's over. I won't let anything bad happen to you.'

*

'Open your eyes, my love. Wake up.'

Martel's voice was excited. For a moment, I misled myself into believing that we were back in our bed, the sunlight playfully caressing my face, the joyful song of the birds surrounding us ... and that nothing bad had happened.

But reality didn't allow me to extend my sweet illusion. I was still in the ship's cabin, and the salty air reminded me of everything I'd lost.

Martel helped me to stand up. My body was stiff from three nights spent on that ship – I hadn't been able to move much, not easily anyway. Around us, euphoria could be felt in the air as the crew chatted cheerfully.

'What's happening?' I asked; my voice was weak.

'Everything is all right,' Martel replied with a soft smile. 'The journey is finally over. We've arrived at our new home.'

I said nothing, nor did he expect me to. Martel understood that I needed time – time to heal, to process. He took my hand firmly and led me forward. As my feet finally stepped on solid ground, I felt a small relief. I'd always loved the sea, but in this moment, I realised I preferred admiring it from the side.

The sight before me was unfamiliar, but enchanting. Capri. In truth, I'd never seen a more beautiful piece of land. The coast was busy with locals trading goods. I could see other islands nearby, like dots on the blue horizon. We were far away from the 'history' of our lives, where the first chapter of our story was left behind in ruins. Here, perhaps, we could begin a new one. I didn't know if I was ready to start a new chapter, but I supposed I didn't have a choice.

We walked, following a man who seemed to know the place well. Holding Martel's hand, I stepped with insecurity, absorbing everything I saw with wide eyes. We went further into the island, and eventually, we stopped in front of a house. It was modest. Martel exchanged a few words with the man who'd led us and handed him a small leather purse, with gold, I assumed.

I was terrified. I'd always thought my family home modest, but this place was no bigger than our horses' stable – it was nothing but a cottage. It was old and looked to have been uninhabited for a long time. I was afraid to cross the threshold – I didn't yet want to see what my new life looked like.

Martel was optimistic, excited even. I wondered where he found the strength to smile, to conceal his own fears that he surely had – everything was just as new to him as it was for me. And yet there he was, determined and hopeful. Was it all for me?

I threw myself into his arms, feeling drained and fragile.

'We'll stay here for a while,' Martel said, 'until we can build something better. Valerio was generous to let us use this place. It's not what you're used to, but we'll make it home.'

I managed a faint smile, and we entered the house. Behind me, the door made a squeaky sound, and I heard Martel mumble that he would fix it. Did he know how to?

'The most important thing is that we are alive. The gods have more plans for us,' he said, and I shivered at the word *alive*. The memories flashed brightly in front of my eyes again – his hands, as strong as steel, wrapped around me, dragging me against my will while the only thing I could do was scream her name.

'We'll find them. I promise!' he assured me, fervently now, holding my face in his hands, but I saw grief in his eyes, same as mine.

That night, as we lay on our simple bed, Martel fell asleep immediately, exhausted by all the stress and effort, doubled because of me. And here came the most difficult part – closing my eyes. Once I did it, it was me and the memory. I saw everything again and again.

The day I sent the letter to Beatricia was the last relatively peaceful one. Young Francesco and Lucretia did not return with my family, nor did I hear from them. That very night, I was awoken by Martel's voice shouting my name.

'Patricia! Wake up, Patricia!'

Confused, I sat up in bed. Martel was running around the room, frantically collecting jewels and coins in a small leather purse. The muffled noise from outside came into focus, chaos streaming through the entire house. Before I could ask what was happening, the doors burst open.

'Master, the ship will leave soon. If you want to live, you'd better hurry!'

One of our servants stood in the doorway, breathless and wide-eyed. His words made no sense to me, but his urgency was obvious. Startled, I'd tried to pull the blanket and cover myself, as a reasonable and decent reaction to a sudden intrusion, but no one was paying attention to me at that moment, and the whole action felt misplaced, more like a comfort from an old world that I felt myself clinging to – worthless now, currency in a dead country, a rock given to someone with thirst.

'Take what you can and wait for us on the shore,' Martel ordered the man.

The servant nodded and vanished down the corridor.

'Martel ...' Panic was beginning to rise in me; I didn't understand what was happening, and yet I knew, and I knew it wouldn't end well.

Martel was by my side in an instant, pulling the blanket from me and grasping my hand tightly.

'They're already here' was all he said, and I knew to whom he was referring.

I shook my head in disbelief. My thoughts flew straight to my family, the three women who had to return to me, to his house.

'No, no, no! I'm not leaving!' My voice was still quiet, but firm.

'Patricia, what are you saying?' Martel's voice rose sharply. 'Do you even understand what's happening? Do you want to die?'

I hardly recognised him. The shadow of fear had transformed his features – there was strength and determination I had never seen before. Despite my instinct to obey him, another force within me was stronger: a mother's love.

'I'm not going anywhere without my daughter!' I said flatly. There was no hesitation, but even I was beginning to hear the unreality of the statement.

I expected him to argue, but the face I loved twisted with remorse, revealing the decision he'd already made, one I hadn't anticipated.

'Forgive me,' he murmured, 'but I won't lose you. This is for the best.'

Before I could respond, his arms wrapped around me. In a moment, I was pulled to my feet.

'No, no, no!' I cried, struggling against him. He didn't seem to hear. His grip didn't loosen. He didn't even bring himself to look at me. He wouldn't leave me behind no matter how much I begged. It was at that moment I realised that everything was ending.

He was pulling me with a force I didn't know he had. His tender hands, which once plucked so lightly at his musical instrument, creating such a magical sound, were now strong, veins visible above the muscles. Against logic, I couldn't bring myself to stop fighting.

My cries echoed through the corridors:

'Beatricia! Beatricia! Beatricia!'

Martel led me through the secret passage we had once used to meet each other. He lit a torch. My resistance had calmed, replaced with shivering and sobbing. I allowed myself to be led, and soon I felt the salty air hit my face. The full moon once again bore witness with an unblinking face. We started running, but the sand made things harder for my already heavy feet.

Shouting and a host of other terrible sounds were coming from the house now. I refused to look back; I just wanted to cover my ears, squeeze my eyes and keep the memory of this place beautiful, as it had always been for me.

Finally, we reached the ship, which had remained hidden behind massive rocks. We pushed away from the shore. It was my first time at sea. My fear deepened as I looked out at the black water merging with the dark sky and felt the waves that swung the ship from side to side – the foundation of my life was being shaken, and now I struggled to even keep my feet under me.

*

The first few days passed swiftly. From sunrise to nightfall, we worked to transform the small house into a cozy nest for two birds who had flown south. I moved through the house, cleaning with a cloth in hand, which Martel found amusing. Truthfully, even I hadn't imagined myself in such a role. Despite my exhaustion and the clear evidence of my lack of natural skill as a housewife, I found the experience oddly intriguing. One of my greatest challenges, however, was attempting to cook.

Our food supplies ran low too quickly. Martel, ever cheerful and good-hearted, soon made acquaintances in the village. He took on the full burden of providing for us, determined to shield me from any hardship. I knew partly he was led by guilt – his belief that he had condemned me to a life far from the comfort I was used to living in. But I reminded him often that he had saved me and that I owed him everything. Neither the luxury I once enjoyed nor the maids who attended me could compare to the life we now shared. But there was something I needed back from my old life – my family.

Martel's skilful hands found purpose again, but not creating music this time – an elderly woodworker, Giuseppe, was in need of help. Soon after, Giuseppe and his wife, Margarita, embraced us as part of their family – their own having also been hollowed out after the tragic loss of their only child. I was astonished by the people in the village. Their sincerity stood in contrast to the hypocrisy of the city I came from. When I set aside thoughts of what had brought us there, I had to admit that I was truly happy. For the first time, I felt I belonged, as though I'd finally found my place in the world. We became part of the little island's humble society, without titles – we were simply Patricia and Martel, bound by the gods in a sacred union and devoted to one another.

Our days fell into a comfortable rhythm, leaving no room for old habits. I began helping Margarita in the forest, where she gathered herbs to sell. She taught me to identify them and shared the secrets of their healing qualities. With all the changes that had happened, with everything that I'd been through in such a short period of time, I was a different Patricia – at least, it felt like it to me. Was it the same for the three women I carried in my heart? I would watch the sea every day, hoping to glimpse an arriving ship that might bring my mother, my daughter and my Lucretia back to me, or at least news of them, but no such ship ever came. A year had passed, and still, I waited.

*

It was a not-so-warm day. With no docked ship on the shore to sell herbs to, I had more time on my hands than usual. I decided to climb a hill that offered a magnificent view of the sea. I walked at a steady pace, but weirdly, my breath became uneven, so I stopped to compose myself. How could I be tired so soon? Lost in thought, I suddenly sensed someone behind me, and as I turned, I saw a woman approaching. She smiled warmly when our eyes met. Her face was radiant, like a little sun, shining when she smiled. Something about her drew me in, an energy so pure it made me want to wait for her.

As she reached me, I could see her skin was indeed flawless, smooth and luminous. She had golden hair that was made to look all the more resplendent by the daylight, and her eyes were a shock of blue. She was, without doubt, the most beautiful woman I had ever seen. I was mesmerised.

'Hello,' she greeted. 'Are you headed to the top?'

'Actually, I am,' I replied, smiling back and wondering if she was out for a walk like me, or perhaps she also collected.

'Mind if I join you?' Her eyes shone with an innocence that made refusal impossible.

'Of course not.'

My answer seemed to delight her, and for some reason, I felt pleased by her happiness. As we walked, I felt she reminded me of someone, but I couldn't quite place the familiarity.

'What's your name?' she asked, breaking the silence.

'Patricia.'

'It suits you – it's a beautiful name.' I found myself feeling embarrassed at her compliment – youth was no longer in my favour, as undoubtedly it was for her.

We continued without speaking, for which I was grateful; my breathing was heavy, and a conversation would have made it worse. When we reached the top, I hurried to sit on the grass, closing my eyes as I inhaled deeply. When I opened them again, she was seated beside me. This didn't bother me, but I was surprised by how silent her movements had been.

The view before us was breathtaking. The sea stretched endlessly, smooth as marble. I buried my fingers in the cool grass.

'It's beautiful,' I said softly.

'What is? The sea?'

'Not just the sea. Everything.'

She nodded thoughtfully before speaking again. 'You see the world differently, Patricia. It's a gift for some and a curse for others. What does it feel like for you?'

Her question startled me, but I thought on it.

'I suppose it's a little of both.'

'A wise answer,' she said, sounding satisfied. It finally struck me. The reason I hadn't been able to place the familiarity I felt with her was because she reminded me of two people – my mother, ever wise, and my daughter, who had inherited the family skills.

'Do you miss someone?' Her words were gentle enough, but they cut straight to the heart of my pain. It was as if she could see right into me.

'Do not be frightened,' she continued, and something had changed in her. Her beauty had sharpened somehow – she was still soft and innocent, but there was something raw there, otherworldly. I was unable to look away. 'We never truly lose those we are connected to. Beatricia has her path to walk, and if neither of you deviate from your course, you will meet again. But remember this: if you focus on the pain, it will only prolong your suffering. Let the past shape you into someone better, not bitter.'

'How do you know all this?' I only managed to whisper as panic had begun rising within me.

'This and many other things are known to me,' she replied with a calm voice. 'For example, you must keep your energy for the child.'

'The child?' I repeated. The thread of our conversation was now completely lost for me.

'The one in your womb.' She made it sound so obvious.

My mouth fell open. My hand moved instinctively to my stomach as if searching for proof.

My child. Mine and Martel's. The fruit of a love so rare, almost divine. How had I not realised? The symptoms should have been obvious – I had experienced them before. Oh, how happy Martel would be! A smile stretched my lips as I imagined his reaction, and I felt a faint blush warming my cheeks. But how did this stranger know?

I looked up, ready to demand answers, but my words caught in my throat as I only saw gold and blue – sun and sea. The grass where she had sat was undisturbed. Trembling with excitement, confusion and an overwhelming mix of unnameable emotions, I stood, clutching my still-flat belly.

It had been so long since the gods had appeared that I thought they'd forgotten me, especially here, on this small island far from home, but they never forget. They miss nothing.

The sky above began to darken with heavy clouds that foretold of a storm. There was no ship on the horizon, and even the birds had vanished, taking shelter. The silence around me was deafening. A drop of rain landed on my face, and suddenly, my heart raced. I felt energy running through me with the overwhelming need to move.

I ran, and even though I moved faster down the hill than I had on the way up, I could not outrun the rain. I was soaked quick and deep, and the downpour proceeded to blur my vision. All I could think of was Martel.

I approached the house, gasping for breath, and I reached the door just as it swung open. Martel stood there as though he had been waiting for me. I threw myself into his arms, my wet face on his, our warm lips together.

*

The days passed quickly, and my belly grew alongside the life in it. We had moved into a new home, a house built by Martel's own hands. It was here that our child would take its first breath. It was here that my life had truly begun again, as it was meant to be.

My perspective had transformed completely. Everywhere I looked, I saw hope, love, and harmony. Yet some things remained the same – I never stopped waiting. Ships came and went, but none brought the news I longed for. Still, I told myself not to despair. They were out there somewhere: my mother, Beatricia and Lucretia …

*

Rafael took his first breath as I struggled to catch mine. His tiny hands reached for me, his cries searching for comfort, and I was there. I held him close, promising that I would never leave him.

I couldn't help but compare the two men I had made fathers. The Prefect had loved Beatricia, but he was never meant to be a father or a husband. He did not understand love, and it showed in every unnatural attempt he made to fill those roles. Martel, on the other hand, adored me and Rafael. He would give his life for his family without hesitation. I could not ask for more.

Life carried on. We were no longer the young musician and the beautiful woman of noble origin. We were simply two people who had survived life's trials, remaining grateful, stronger and still deeply in love.

Martel gave me a home, built with labour and sweat, and I gave him a son, born of love.

Everything in our life was love.

*

Rafael found me on the shore, gazing at the vast sea as the sun set. He wrapped his arms comfortably around my shoulders.

'Mother, why are you here again?' he asked, as if he hadn't already asked countless times, as if he didn't know my answer.

'I'm looking at the sea, son.' My voice had changed with the years, but it still carried the weight of unspoken sorrow.

'You see it every day. We live here,' he said gently, challenging me. 'I think there's more to it than that.

Something else brings you here, and I think it's what makes you sad.'

I sighed and cupped his face in my hands. My little boy had grown into a wise young man. He deserved to know the truth, yet fear wouldn't let me speak of my pain – what if he began waiting too? What if Beatricia never appeared?

Pain twisted inside me, and I clutched my chest as I fought to steady my breath.

'Mother, let me bring you home.' Worried, Rafael guided me gently towards the house.

Martel waited for us on the threshold, and his smile was like a balm to my uneasy heart. The years had changed us both, but the bond between us remained as unbreakable as the day we met.

I turned to Rafael. 'I want to tell you something, my son.'

'I'm here.'

'From the moment I first met your father, I saw everything – our entire story. I saw us grow old together, even this moment right now. In that instant, I knew that life made no sense without him.'

Rafael's eyes glistened. 'Mother, your love is extraordinary. I hope to find something as beautiful one day.'

'Never wish for someone else's path,' I advised him. 'But trust that your own will bring you happiness. Luck runs in our family.' I smiled and kissed his forehead.

As I walked inside the house, I overheard Rafael whisper to his father about finding me on the shore again. Martel said nothing. He had carried my grief alongside me for years, and though it burdened us both, his love never weakened.

The evening came quickly, and I laid my tired body on the bed. Next to me, Martel reached out and touched my hand, his breath already heavy and slow, a sure sign he was falling asleep. I wanted to do the same, but something stopped me from doing so. Memories began to overwhelm me – vivid moments from my life appeared like fleeting mirages. My life had been so colourful, full of experiences that most people would scarcely believe possible. My body no longer possessed the strength to cope with the overwhelming emotion and it suddenly trembled. I felt fear – was this it? The end of me? I tried to reach Martel, but my hand refused to obey my mind. A strange feeling spread through me, as though I were slipping into a dream, but I knew that wasn't possible – I was far too tense. The memories swirled, faster and faster before my eyes. Shapes became indistinct, and nothing made sense. I wanted to scream, to cry out for help, but whom would I scream for?

There was fog and space, vast, dense, unknown, and familiar.

*

Beep-beep-beep.

I opened my eyes, confused, and instinctively stretched out to turn off the alarm. Another working day. I had no desire to leave the comfort of my warm, soft bed. Searching blindly, my hand found his. Martin was sleeping quietly beside me, and I leaned closer to embrace him.

His skin was soft and warm, and I wished I could stay there in bed with him all day. Most couples seemed to lose their affection after a few years, but not us. Our love remained as strong as the day we met – filled with emotion, excitement, and desire. Perhaps we were simply lucky. It felt like more than love; it was harmony, a complete and profound connection.

Often I questioned if I deserved such happiness. Why didn't everyone have this? What made us different? So many couples begin with harmony but soon have fights, mistrust and jealousy.

'Good morning, love,' Martin greeted me with a dreamy smile and half-opened eyes.

'Good morning. I hope I didn't wake you with this awful alarm.' I leaned in to kiss him.

'I can't sleep all morning – it's good to get a jump on things,' he said. His expression then fell as he looked at me. 'Is everything alright?'

'Yes, just … those dreams again. You know, the ones that feel so real you wake up disoriented.'

'What was it this time?' Martin asked, patient and attentive as always.

'It wasn't a nightmare, just … intriguing. I can hardly remember it now. Mostly the feeling it left me with,' I frowned. 'But I'm pretty sure it had something to do with Italy from a long way back …'

'Ah, Italy. Next time, sleep calm; I promise our next holiday will be there.' Martin seemed entertained.

'Maybe you're right,' I said thoughtfully. 'I want to visit Italy so badly, and my mind is playing it out in my sleep.' It actually made sense. But I couldn't shake the feeling of a space in my heart, like there was something I was looking for, waiting for. I sighed heavily and stood up with reluctance to prepare for work.

One hour later, I kissed Martin goodbye and marched out in a rush, as always. But as I got into my car, I realised I'd forgotten my coffee thermos on the kitchen table. I had no time to go back – I'd have to buy a coffee on the way.

There was a small café on the main street where I stopped and jumped out of the car. As I opened the door to step inside, I nearly stumbled into some woman who I quickly realised was the last in a long queue. Frustrated, I considered leaving, but my need for caffeine was stronger.

The woman in front of me began walking away, having apparently given up.

'Unbelievable! They put a new girl on duty during the busiest time. I'll write a complaint!' she murmured loudly as she stormed out dramatically.

Curious, I peeked ahead and saw the sure signs of chaos behind the counter. Staff rushed to fill orders, and at the centre of it all was the 'new girl'. Her wide eyes and accent betrayed her nervousness. When finally it was my turn, I stepped forward.

'For you?' she asked. Her almond-shaped eyes and golden hair were striking. But it wasn't her beauty that left me speechless. Something about her felt ... familiar.

'Espresso to go, please,' I finally managed to say. Glancing at the badge on her uniform. Was that the Italian flag? *A strange coincidence*, I thought, as she handed me my coffee.

'Have a nice day,' she said, already turning to the next customer.

Why had this girl made such an impression on me? As I reached the door, my attention was caught by a conversation between two women who, unlike me, had time to sit with their coffee this morning.

'... and I told her, when it's meant to be, people's paths will cross again ...'

Perhaps, I'd return here for a coffee someday. Grasping the door handle, I stepped out with the woman's words echoing in my mind.

CHAPTER III

LIFE

**'When you have been taught to believe
in unreality all your life, it will be very difficult for
you to believe in reality afterwards ...'**
proverb

Betty was covered in sweat and breathing heavily as she opened her eyes. The summer night was warm, but the drops on her forehead weren't from the heat. She reached for the glass of water on her bedside table, took a sip, and sighed. Falling back asleep would be difficult after waking this way, especially after one of *those dreams*.

Betty switched on the small lamp beside her bed, letting its soft glow illuminate the room and steady her thoughts.

'What will I do with these dreams ...?' she murmured, rubbing her temples. Eventually, she lay back into the soft bed and focused her gaze out the window, following the gentle movement of the tree branches pushed by the night breeze.

In the morning, Betty awoke far from refreshed, with only a vague memory of her dream. She felt worried, which wasn't exactly uncommon after a night like the one she'd had. Today, however, was different – she had a plan.

Betty quickly dressed, putting on her old jeans and a T-shirt, and headed to the kitchen for breakfast. Her mother, Carlotta, sat with an empty coffee mug. Her father, Giovanni, had already left for work.

'Betty, what time is it? Are you just waking up now?' Carlotta started with her usual speech. A simple *good morning* would have been nice. 'You'll sleep your life away!'

'I didn't sleep well,' Betty said, attempting to defend herself as she reached for a slice of bread and the jam jar.

'Your usual excuse. You need a new one, or better yet, you can grow up!' Carlotta's voice climbed to an irritating pitch. Betty barely listened; after nineteen years, she'd learned to tune out these dramatic performances.

Betty wasn't ungrateful. Her parents had provided her with a stable life: food, a roof over her head, and as the only child, she got the occasional indulgence. But the house always felt cold; her father didn't seem to have the right to make any decisions in this family, and her mother behaved more like a dictator – the warmth of love was absent, and Betty never really felt like she belonged as a result. She had long since dreamed of leaving, of taking charge of her own destiny, free from her controlling mother. She had just graduated high school, and her parents were pushing her to choose a university, but all she wanted was to pack her bags, find work, and build a life on her own terms.

'… You're wandering without any purpose. Have you even decided on a university?' Carlotta demanded. 'Your father and I are waiting to have some good news for the rest of the family, for once. Are you even listening to me?'

'Hmm? What?' Betty snapped out of her daze.

'Beatricia!' Carlotta threw up her hands. 'One day, I swear, you'll be the death of me!'

'Mom,' Betty sighed, shutting her eyes and counting to five to keep calm. 'Please, relax. I'm still thinking about it.'

'How long do you need to think? Deadlines for applications are soon!'

Betty shrugged, getting up to wash her plate.

'And where do you think you're going?' Carlotta frowned, noting that I was about to leave.

'I'm meeting Vittoria. We're discussing university options,' Betty lied smoothly.

Her mother snorted, but there was nothing more she could say to that, so she waved her hand dismissively.

Betty hid a smile and grabbed her bag. As she stepped out of the house, she immediately pulled out her phone and called Vittoria.

'Hey, Betty! Did you manage to escape?' Vittoria's voice was so refreshingly cheerful.

'Mission accomplished,' Betty replied, grinning. 'I'll meet you at the square.'

Betty could barely hold her excitement as she waited for Vittoria. Today, she would do something bold, something she had never imagined herself doing. Curiosity drove her, but also desperation, and hope. It all started as a joke her friend had made in passing, but over time it had taken root in Betty's mind, until she simply had to do it.

Both girls had lives that most people would consider ordinary. They had lived, for as long as they could remember, in a small town in northern Italy – it was no place for an ambitious young girl full of dreams and ideas. The difference between Betty and every other girl her age living in her town was that she felt out of place. While everyone else seemed content with what they had in front of them, she sought something new. She didn't want to follow the typical pattern and wake up at the age of sixty realising she'd never actually lived. She wanted to taste the different flavours life could offer, and she had the courage to try.

But courage, curiosity, and her other drivers weren't the only things pushing her forwards today. She had a secret – one only her closest friend knew. Betty's dreams weren't ordinary; they haunted her, vivid and puzzling, filled with emotions that felt real yet foreign. She'd done her research, reading books and articles and whatever else she could find, but she couldn't find the answer to her key question: what did her dreams mean? She couldn't accept that they were simply the result of repressed fears and a wandering imagination – there was something more to them. She needed to know.

Walking side by side with Leticia, Betty felt a mix of emotions as they approached Dr Santini's office, a psychologist who would perform a regression session. Worst case, she would lose a bit of her savings – and she could earn more money as soon as she started working.

'Are you sure about this?' Vittoria asked, looking nervous and full of doubt – this was no longer a joke. 'I mean, what if something goes wrong? Like … what if you don't wake up?' Vittoria bit her lip, horrified by the idea, as her friend rolled her eyes.

'If my brain gets fried, it won't be much of a disappointment to my mother – she already thinks I'm hopeless.' Betty laughed.

Vittoria groaned but followed her friend. The two girls exchanged a reassuring look as they rang the bell at the door to the doctor's office. They were let in by a young woman with a polite smile, dressed smart.

'Welcome to Dr Santini's office. She will see you shortly. Would you like tea or coffee in the meantime?'

'No, thank you.' Betty shook her head, too nervous to put anything in her stomach at that moment.

'Actually … for me, tea, please,' Vittoria said, clearing her throat.

The secretary nodded and vanished, leaving them alone in the waiting room.

'How long do you think this will take?' Betty's voice was impatient.

'I have no idea. It depends, I suppose,' Vittoria replied, shrugging. 'Don't worry though – I'll just go through all the magazines.' She grabbed one off the top of a glossy stack on a side table and settled into the sofa.

'Thank you for being here with me. I don't think I could do this alone,' Betty admitted.

'We're friends. I'll always be here for you – even for crazy ideas like this one,' Vittoria said with a laugh, though secretly, she hoped this would be their last wild adventure. She wished for simpler days, doing the things other girls their age did.

'Here's your tea,' the secretary said, appearing again with a steaming mug that she handed off to Vittoria. 'And you, miss,' she said, turning to Betty, 'you may go in now. Dr Santini is ready for you.'

Betty stood and approached the door the secretary had pointed to, trying her best to keep herself calm: *nothing to be afraid of, nothing to be afraid of ...* She gripped the door handle with trembling fingers. When she pushed it open, Betty found herself in a small office, but beautifully arranged. Two armchairs faced each other, a large desk stood in the centre, and a vibrant potted plants filled every corner. The curtain had been drawn back, and sunlight streamed through. The place felt inviting.

Behind the desk stood a middle-aged woman dressed in a sharp suit and high heels. Her face radiated a warmth that immediately set Betty at ease; her welcoming smile seemed capable of dismissing any fear.

'Hi, Betty! Come in. I'm Valeria.' She gestured towards the sofa. 'Make yourself comfortable. How are you feeling today?'

Betty sat down as directed. 'Fine ... I guess I'm a little nervous,' she confessed, playing with the ring on her right hand.

'What worries you the most?' Valeria asked with a calm and patient tone as she moved to the armchair across Betty.

'Well ... I've never done anything like this before. I'm not sure what to expect.' She glanced down at her lap.

'This session is entirely for your benefit and happens at your pace. You're in control. Whether you want to go ahead with the procedure or just have a chat today, the choice is yours. The aim is to make you feel as comfortable and secure as possible, and everything shared here stays confidential.'

Betty knew she had come too far to turn back now. Answers to the questions that had haunted her were within reach.

'I'm ready.'

'Excellent. Let me walk you through the procedure first, so you know exactly what to expect. It's a very safe and straightforward process.' Valeria's tone remained calm and reassuring as she detailed each step of the regression session.

Betty listened carefully, nodding along.

'Any questions?'

'Not yet,' Betty replied. 'But I might have some later.'

'Of course. Feel free to ask anytime. Now, please lie down on the sofa. Make yourself comfortable. Close your eyes, and let all tension drain from your mind.'

Betty followed the instructions and tried to imagine she was at home, sinking into her bed. Still, her heart fluttered with nervous anticipation.

'I'm going to count to ten,' Valeria said softly. 'With each number, you'll feel more relaxed, and your mind will drift. By the time I reach ten, you'll return to your last dream. Ready? One … two … three …'

Betty had seen it in movies, but she could never understand how this all worked. Whatever the trick was, it worked on her, too. She felt her body automatically preparing for a sleep, as if she had given it a command. Her thoughts began floating as the doctor's voice grew somewhat distant. There were now colours and figures becoming clearer and clearer in her mind.

'Describe what you see,' Valeria's voice gently nudged.

'A house,' Betty began. 'I'm in a house. It's large, spacious, and … empty. The emptiness feels suffocating. I feel so alone. It's evening. I'm dressed strangely. The house looks ancient, old, but elegant. I'm shivering, though it's not from cold. There's this terrible sense of grief, like I've lost someone important … but I know even more loss is coming …'

… Someone was knocking at the door – a loud, impatient pounding that filled the house with tension. The servant hurried to answer, and I followed close behind with uneasiness tightening in my chest. Something was wrong. It was far too late for a visit.

Before the servant reached the door, I caught her hand to stop her. Pressing a finger to my lips, I leaned in so she could hear my whisper, 'Don't open it until you're sure who it is.'

She nodded, and her eyes reflected my anxiety.

The knocking came again, harder this time, making the heavy door tremble. We exchanged a worried glance as a desperate male voice called from the other side.

'Oh gods, open up, or it'll be the end of us all!'

The voice was unfamiliar, yet something in that moment convinced me the real danger wasn't coming from the stranger outside, but that there was a threat already upon us.

'Open it,' I said, despite the fear twisting inside me.

The servant hesitated but obeyed, pulling the heavy door open. She gasped as a figure stepped into view.

'Lucretia! Is it really you?' I couldn't believe it. She hugged me tightly, and behind her stood a young man I didn't recognise.

'We must leave,' were her first words. Her voice was urgent and commanding. 'Your mother sent us. Francesco and I barely made it into the city. The streets are dangerous, but worse is coming.'

'What are you talking about?' I asked, unable to hide my disbelief.

'She speaks the truth,' the young man interrupted, and his intense gaze locked with mine. His eyes seemed to pierce through me – I felt as if I'd been stung. He looked to be about my age, yet his body bore the strength of a man hardened by labour. His black hair was now dusty and ruffled by the long ride, but he was clearly handsome. His look showed that he was on a mission, and he was determined not to fail.

'I have a letter from your mother,' Lucretia said, pulling a sealed parchment from her satchel.

'There's no time for letters,' Francesco snapped. 'We have to leave now!'

'My grandmother is in bed,' I said with a trembling voice as the full gravity of the moment began to sink in. 'Her health is fragile. She won't survive such a journey.'

Tears filled my eyes. Grandmother's bad health was something I hadn't told my mother about yet, knowing it would break her heart. Lucretia placed a comforting hand on mine. She understood the weight of my sorrow.

'We'll carry her if we must!' Francesco said sharply. He sounded like a soldier – someone who could make the impossible happen.

'Beatricia, trust him,' Lucretia urged with a spark of determination. 'He serves your mother, and he'll keep us safe.' There was no point in arguing further. Time was slipping through our fingers like sand, and I nodded in agreement.

Convincing my grandmother to leave was no small task. Nobly, she had insisted on staying behind, unwilling to risk our lives for her sake. But I refused to go without her.

When Francesco entered her room with cloaks for us so we wouldn't be easily recognised, something changed. Agostina's sharp gaze lingered on him, studying him in a way only she could. Whatever she saw in him for that brief second made her change her mind.

'Here, let's cover you properly,' Lucretia said as she helped wrap me in the dark, heavy fabric. Her hands trembled slightly, but I could tell she was trying to keep her voice steady for my sake. Tears slipped down my cheeks, falling onto her hands as she adjusted the cloak around me. She said nothing, but the look in her eyes mirrored my own feelings – grief, fear, and the unshakable certainty that something terrible was coming.

Screams and shouts could be heard now, drawing closer to the house. Still, I couldn't understand what was happening, but I knew that we had to make it safely to my mother's estate. I missed her so much, and I was so afraid …

Two horses waited for us in the courtyard. Suddenly, Grandmother grasped my arm and spoke with her frail voice.

'Beatricia, you must ride with Francesco.'

I looked at her, stunned. Her request made no sense to me. Lucretia had arrived with him, so they could ride back together. I had no intention to separate from my grandmother.

'But—' I tried objecting but she squeezed my arm with surprising strength and her voice grew firm.

'You must go with him!'

Lucretia had already climbed on one of the horses, and Francesco helped my grandmother onto the saddle behind her.

'Time is precious, Beatricia,' Lucretia said.

Before I could fully process what was happening, Francesco's arms were around my waist, lifting me onto the other horse with ease. His touch burned like fire against my skin, and my heart pounded, though not from fear.

My discomfort at our closeness faded quickly, replaced with terror as we found ourselves off the grounds. The streets were unrecognisable, painted with blood everywhere I looked. The cries of the dying ran through the air, mingling with the scent of smoke. Death lurked on every corner. I wanted to close my eyes and not open them until we'd arrived at my mother's house, but I couldn't even command my eyelids to shut. This was a sight I would never forget.

Suddenly we stopped.

'We can't take the same path I used to get here – it's completely blocked!' Francesco said in frustration. He hadn't expected things to escalate so quickly. Yet, despite his momentary despair, his gaze hadn't faltered – he had a young man's desire to prove himself. I felt safer looking at him.

'What do we do now?' I asked. 'Lucretia, what—' I turned to seek her guidance, but my words froze in my throat. They were gone. 'Lucretia!' I shouted, almost crying.

'Keep quiet,' Francesco hissed. 'We can't risk attracting attention. We'll go back for them – they can't have gone far.'

He spurred the horse back along the path we'd taken, and every passing moment weighed heavier and heavier on my chest. Despair itself sought to suffocate me.

Then we heard it – a faint groan. Francesco nudged the horse closer, and my stomach twisted at what we found. There, on the ground, lay Lucretia and my grandmother, their clothes stained with blood. My breath caught. Without thinking, I jumped off the horse and ran to them, falling to my knees beside my grandmother. Her lifeless body lay motionless before me as I caressed her face. I choked on my tears; the reality was too much to bear.

'Francesco,' a weak voice gasped behind me. I turned towards Lucretia. She was still alive, though only barely. Francesco knelt beside her with a face etched with anguish.

'Protect her … with your life,' she whispered.

He only nodded, his jaw clenched as the flickering glow of distant fires illuminated his grim expression. He reached out and gently closed her eyes. They would never open again.

'No, no!' I cried, overwhelmed by the sudden slap of grief. Lucretia, who was like a second mother to me, was gone. And her last words, addressed to this stranger, assigned him a great task – my life.

I leaned over Lucretia's body, wanting to hold her one last time, but Francesco's arms wrapped around me once again and pulled me away. I resisted as he rushed me back to the horse. I struggled with all the strength I had left.

'Let me go!'

'I won't let anything happen to you.' His voice broke through my sobs. 'You're safe with me.'

The words echoed in my ears, but the only comfort I felt came the moment I fell into the darkness of unconsciousness.

When I opened my eyes, warmth pressed against my back, and I realised I was cradled in Francesco's arms. The soft rhythm of the horse's steps comforted me, though the memories quickly flooded back, depriving me of any true sense of peace.

'How do you feel?' Francesco said. I both heard and felt his voice as I leaned into him.

I turned slightly, meeting his gaze. His exhaustion showed. In the daylight, he appeared more like the boy he was – not the man who had faced death beside me.

'Where are we?' I asked. I was surprised by how quiet my voice sounded.

'Somewhere north,' he said with a sigh. 'I'm not certain exactly where.'

'North? But … mother's estate is south.'

'The roads south were blocked.' His voice was hard. 'Had we gone that way, we wouldn't have survived the night. I had no choice but to head in the opposite direction – away from the city, somewhere safe where we can wait for this storm to pass.'

I tried to understand his reasoning, but the weight of the situation was too much for me. Words of gratitude were buried beneath grief and loss. I wanted to blame him – it felt easier – but deep down, I knew he'd made the only choice he could. Still, the pain was raw, too consuming for words.

So I stayed silent, letting him guide me. My world had crumbled, and I no longer had the strength to question the gods. I left myself to his care, and wherever the path ahead might lead.

Days passed in a blur. We stopped only for essentials and never stayed in one place long. Francesco believed that the farther we fled, the safer we'd be. The towns we passed through were quiet, untouched by the violence we'd left behind. I found no peace in the silence – I found no peace.

Francesco spoke of the gods sparing our lives, but I couldn't share his faith. To me, our survival felt more like abandonment. I was a shadow, a shade in the light of day. Had it not been for Francesco's persistence, I wouldn't have eaten or taken water.

We finally stopped again, just inside the limits of a small town. Francesco helped me off the horse, making sure that I was firmly on the ground before removing his hands from me. I was already used to his closeness – it had been a necessity. Under different circumstances, the intimacy we'd already shared would have been unthinkable, scandalous even. Yet here we were, strangers bound by survival. And though I couldn't understand his devotion, I recognised the care in his actions. Francesco wasn't just fulfilling a duty; he was determined to protect me, even at his own expense. For the first time in days, I found myself wondering why.

'Stay here. I'll be back soon,' Francesco said. I nodded. He took a step forward, then hesitated. Turning back, he gently pulled the hood of my cloak up over my head.

'For safety,' he added, then disappeared off into the crowd.

I stood at the edge of a quiet street, overlooking the bustling square. The day promised sunshine, but the crisp morning breeze made me wrap my arms around myself. The air was laden with the scents of market stalls – fresh bread and fish.

My gaze wandered aimlessly, not focusing on anything specific. I tried to lose myself in the view before me, desperate to distract myself from the weight of my thoughts. Time no longer felt real; since that terrible night, it seemed to have stopped. I had no idea how long we'd been travelling, or how long I'd been standing there.

When Francesco's voice broke through my oblivious state, I jumped in fright.

'It's me,' he said. He was smiling wide. There looked to be actual joy in his expression and the site was baffling. 'I have good news – our wandering is finally over. We'll stay here, in the house of a widow. She's all alone and has little to offer, but her generosity means everything to us right now.'

I wished I could share in his happiness. In the few days we'd travelled together, Francesco had become someone whose company I found oddly comforting. Under different circumstances, I might have even been curious to know him better.

But now, with my soul still drowning in sorrow, I couldn't bring a smile to my face. But I did manage to rouse my voice.

'And what would two strangers do in the house of this woman?' I asked, sharper than I'd intended – I felt clumsy speaking, thinking about pitch and lips, things that used to simply fall into place.

His smile faded and I instantly felt guilt. But I couldn't seem to control myself. I was caught in an endless battle between what I knew was right and the overwhelming grief that clouded my judgment.

'We'll help her however we can,' Francesco replied. The disappointment in his voice did not go unnoticed by me. 'I can't offer you anything better right now, but I promise you'll be safe.'

'Lead the way,' I said quietly. I wished to say more – to apologise, to thank him – but my thoughts were a mess.

We walked in silence. I paid no attention to the streets we passed or the town that would now be my home. My interest in the world around me had disappeared, making me, once again, nothing but a shadow trailing after Francesco.

Eventually, we stopped in front of a small house – modest. Before knocking, Francesco turned to me with a heavy expression.

'I need to tell you something,' he said, his face visibly struggling with the words he still held. 'I couldn't tell her who we really are or where we're from. This situation demands … discretion. I told her we're a family in need of work.'

His words hung in the air as I processed them. My cheeks blushed, and I looked down, unable to keep my eyes on his.

'Inappropriate and false,' I said. I could feel the chill of my own voice. 'But what's done is done. We have no choice but to stick to your story, as long as it is just a story.'

The widow greeted us warmly. She was kind, good-hearted, and generous, despite her unassuming life. She told us her husband had passed years ago, and she had no children to care for her.

'The gods didn't bless us with children,' she said with a sad smile. 'But we accepted their will. Something else was destined for us.'

Her kindness was humbling, yet it stirred a bitter thought in me: *good people were not always happy, and happiness was not always given to those who deserved it.*

That night, as I arranged the room we were to share as a husband and wife, Francesco approached me. He looked like someone walking up to a horse that had just bucked them off.

'I want to give you something.'

He held a folded parchment. My breath caught – it was the letter from my mother, the one I'd never had the chance to read. His eyes filled with sorrow, but I couldn't bear his pity.

Taking the letter, I sat down with trembling hands and impatience. I'd waited days to read it, but even a few seconds more felt unbearable at that moment. As I unfolded it, I saw the rush with which my mother had written the letter:

My sun, my joy, my life, my Beatricia! We have lost
too much to suffer another tragedy. I beg you,
as soon as you receive this letter, prepare for an
immediate journey. No sleep or peace will come
to me until I can hold you again. You will
always be a part of me. I love you.
Your mother.

I couldn't hold back any longer and burst into tears. I felt regret for having rushed to read the letter, for now it was read – the final words my mother would give to me. Was it possible to hold on to hope when my entire world had been shattered, when the earth had crumbled beneath my feet and the sky itself seemed to weigh on my shoulders?

A hand rested gently on my back, a calming weight. This man, a stranger only days ago, who now had his freedom, chose to remain loyal to my family – to me. Francesco's desire to help came not from obligation but from kindness. I owed him more than I could ever repay, and I would continue to depend on him in the future. For me, the life ahead was like a fog through which I couldn't see, but there was still some luck by my side, a beam of light piercing through the darkness – Francesco. He would stand by me and protect me; I was certain of it by the look in his eyes.

I wiped away my tears and searched for his gaze.

'I'm grateful you came into my life,' I said. 'I'll wait until it's safe, and then I'll go back to search for my mother. She's the only thing left of my old life. From now on, I won't be Beatricia with a high title, nor will you be Francesco, the servant. Here, we'll be whoever we want to be, and we'll try to find happiness.'

He smiled, a small but genuine expression, and I knew my words had touched him.

'As I've promised to protect you,' he said softly, 'I promise now that when the time comes, I'll be by your side in your search for your mother. But I have one request. Be patient, no matter how hard it is. I know she'd rather you stay alive somewhere, waiting, than lose you because you acted too soon.'

I nodded, simply because words weren't necessary – it was no longer grief that held my tongue.

The days passed slowly at first, with each moment weighed down by the effort of adjusting to our new life. But as I started getting used to it, time began to slip by more easily. Months passed. The first thing I took care of in the widow's house was the garden. Neglected when we arrived, it now brimmed with life – the blossoming flowers brought joy to my eyes.

I often found myself lost in thought as I worked in the garden. Life was a curious thing: calm like the sea that then erupts into a storm. Storms destroyed everything in their path, but they also spared lives, offering second chances. And that was how I started feeling – spared. Slowly, I began to smile again.

During the day, I helped the widow, who was happy to have someone to talk to. Francesco worked hard, and I rarely saw him until evening. Dinner became my favourite time of day. Francesco would entertain us with stories; his natural charisma and humour lifted the weight of sorrow from our hearts, even if only for a short while.

After dinner, Francesco would go to the room we shared and fall asleep almost instantly, exhausted from the day's labour. At first, this was a relief for me. Sharing a room with him had felt strange enough – though he'd made it more bearable by electing to sleep on a blanket on the floor in the far corner, far from the comfortable bed where I slept – but as time passed, I found myself wishing for more. I wanted him to stay awake because I wanted to know him better. I wanted to talk to him, to watch his smile and feel its warmth. Yet he kept a polite distance – a distance I suddenly had the desire to shorten.

One evening, as I finished my work in the kitchen, I noticed Francesco heading to the garden instead of our room. Curious, I left everything and followed him. I found him leaning against a tree, his arms wrapped around himself. His expression looked troubled. I couldn't bear seeing him this way; he was my beam of light.

For a brief moment before stepping closer, I allowed my eyes to enjoy the sight of him. He was much taller than me, his frame strong, yet there was a softness to him, something almost childlike. His dark hair begged to be touched, and his hands were a contradiction – rough and work-worn but inviting and warm. My thoughts began to run ahead of me, to more intimate things.

'Is everything alright?' I asked, finally coming up beside him. Here, in the garden, all alone with the sun having almost set, the tension I felt made me struggle for air.

He didn't look at me. 'I'm just enjoying the garden.'

His refusal to meet my gaze stung. I wanted him to look at me. I craved it, though I wasn't sure if it was right to crave it.

'It's a joy for the eyes,' I replied, grasping for words.

Regret began to creep in. I shouldn't have followed him. I felt I should leave and pretend I hadn't interrupted him.

'There are things that bring more joy to my eyes in this house,' he said softly.

His words caught my breath. I didn't want to move – I only wanted him to keep speaking.

'Unfortunately,' he continued, 'my eyes aren't allowed to enjoy anything else but this garden.'

His voice fell, and my heart felt both joy and sorrow. His words were a gift – intimate, tender, and meant only for me. Yet something held him back, and I believed I knew what it was – I at least had some ideas. He thought me beyond his reach because of my origin, or he didn't care about my roots and instead felt guilty for the circumstances under which we'd been brought together.

It was difficult to know exactly, but I needed to show him otherwise.

I took a step closer. He finally turned to face me, and our eyes met. The tension between us grew, unspoken but undeniable. Timidly, he raised a hand to brush the side of my face. I leaned into his touch, closing my eyes.

And then I felt his lips on mine.

*

It was early autumn, and the heat in town seemed not to want to leave. The years I'd spent there had made me love it as my own. The weight of my past – the memories haunting my dreams and the pain that stabbed my heart – had eased, allowing me to live my new life. But deep down, I knew it was all still there.

'My love, I have wonderful news,' Francesco called out as he arrived home. I was sitting in the sunlight, combing the chestnut hair of our little Akadia, the child the gods had blessed us with a few years ago. As always, Francesco greeted her first with a kiss on the forehead.

'Speak, then, so I can share the joy,' I replied cheerfully.

He wrapped an arm around my waist, pulling me close. His voice carried a trace of tension as he continued. 'Today, I met a merchant, a good man. He's headed south to trade, and I learned he'll be travelling as far as your town.

My hands froze in Akadia's hair.

'I've arranged for him to bring me news,' he went on, carefully watching my reaction. 'I described the estate by the sea and promised him a good reward if he returned with information.'

I couldn't speak, couldn't hold back the tears. I buried my face in my hands. I had waited so long that I'd nearly forgotten what hope felt like. Yet here he was, Francesco, once again fulfilling his promise to me. He'd promised to protect me, but he had given me so much more – happiness, family, and love. And now, he was keeping his word to help me find my mother.

I couldn't tell if my tears fell out of joy or sadness; the emotions were so overwhelming.

'Mother, mother.' Akadia's wide, frightened eyes searched mine.

'Your mother is very happy, my little flower. Don't be afraid,' Francesco said, taking the comb from my hands and continuing with her hair.

That night, I couldn't close my eyes. Memories of everything I'd been through swirled in my mind. I was amazed at how life had taken such an unexpected turn. The night I thought I'd lost everything, I'd also gained everything – though it took me years to see it that way. Francesco had been the turning point, the light in my darkest hour.

When I first arrived in this town, I couldn't imagine ever finding happiness here. I had walked its streets hidden under the hood of my cloak, unable to bear the sight of anything around me. I had crossed the threshold of the widow's house in search of shelter in exchange for my hands, unused to labour. Yet, in time, this very house became my home. The widow, in gratitude for our care, had left it to us when she passed away.

I was raising my child here. I had found peace here. And now it was time for the last missing piece – news of my mother, Patricia.

Hope blossomed in me like the trees in spring. But a small voice in the back of my mind – persistent as an insect buzzing in my ear – whispered, *What if she isn't there? What if she's gone?*

I refused to listen. Not now. Not when hope had finally returned.

The days crawled by mercilessly slowly. I waited for the merchant's return, restless and unable to focus on anything else. Finally, the day arrived when Francesco would meet him. I stayed at home, pacing from room to room in anticipation.

Nothing could soothe me. Eventually, I sat by the window, looking at the street.

When I saw Francesco in the distance, my heart leapt. Even in a crowded street, I could recognise him instantly. Without thinking, I rushed to the door and ran outside. Our eyes met, and at that moment, I knew. I didn't need to ask. I turned and ran back inside.

Francesco found me in the garden, tears falling freeling, whaling. Silently, he sat beside me on the grass and reached out to rest a hand on me. For a while, we stayed like that, not speaking. What was there to say?

'The man I asked to help brought news today,' he finally spoke. 'He rode to the seaside, but ... there was no one there. The house was destroyed, abandoned like so many we saw that terrible night.'

I felt my chest tighten as he paused.

'But that doesn't mean she didn't survive, my love,' he continued firmly. 'Don't lose hope. She might be out there, alive, longing for you just as you long for her. She probably suffers the same way, wondering why she never heard from you after sending the letter.'

He was right. My mother had always taught me to hold on to faith, hope, and love. Francesco had done everything in his power to help – more than I could ever have asked.

I wiped my tears, but deep inside, that small, insistent voice whispered: *She's gone. You've lost her forever ...*

... Betty opened her eyes, breathing heavily. She was in the office of Dr Santini, who was sitting on the sofa, looking at her with a calm smile.

'Is everything alright, Betty? How do you feel?' she asked with slight concern as she noticed her young patient's confused expression.

Betty didn't answer immediately. How could she? Everything she had seen in her head felt vivid and real yet presented like a dream. The most important thing was that the answers she had so desperately sought for years now began to pour over her like summer rain. Everything was coming into view, falling into place.

She stood abruptly from the couch where she had just relived the story of her past life, excitement suddenly pulsing through her. 'Yes, everything is … more than fine. But now, I really must go.'

Before Dr Santini could respond, Betty grabbed her bag and dug through it to get the money for the session.

'But why so fast?' Dr Santini asked, startled. 'We need to discuss what you've just experienced and—'

Betty had already left the money on the desk and was halfway out the door.

'Maybe some other time,' she said quickly. Just before closing the door behind her, she turned. 'Thank you. You've really helped me.'

Dr Santini blinked in surprise – it was too late to stop her.

'Betty, what happened in there?' Vittoria asked breathlessly, trying to keep up with her friend. Betty had stormed out of the office and was now rushing down the street as though someone were chasing her. 'Betty, wait! Where are we going?'

Suddenly, Betty stopped and turned to face Vittoria. Grabbing her friend's hands, she held them tightly, just as she used to when sharing secrets.

Her intense gaze left Vittoria frozen with worry. *What if something went wrong during the session? What if Betty went crazy?* But Betty's face was glowing with happiness, not madness.

'Vittoria,' Betty said, unable to control her excitement. 'You have to help me with one last thing …'

The next morning, Betty surprised her parents by appearing in the kitchen unusually early.

'Oh, Giovanni, look at this!' her mother exclaimed in mock astonishment. 'Your daughter can actually start her day at a normal hour like the rest of the world.'

Betty didn't respond, nor did she seem bothered. She was smiling – a bright and genuine smile her parents rarely saw.

'And she's in a good mood, too,' her mother jeered. 'Does this have anything to do with the news we're waiting for? Which university have you chosen?'

'You're right – I do have news.'

'That's wonderful, sweetheart,' her father said, glancing at his watch. 'But could you tell us quickly? I need to leave for work.' He stood by the kitchen door with coffee in hand while her mother sat in her bathrobe, cigarette in hand.

'I'm leaving for London today,' Betty said cheerfully, pointing to a packed rucksack in the corner, which had gone unnoticed until now.

Her mother let out a muffled scream, covering her mouth with both hands; meanwhile, her father's mug slipped from his grasp and shattered on the floor.

*

'Patty, I swear, there's nothing more exciting than planning a wedding! And not just any wedding – your best friend's wedding!' Lucy said as she flipped through a glossy bridal magazine. 'I wish mine could be next, but Ben is too scared to take the leap. Honestly, I might just propose to him myself. This world's upside down anyway – why not?'

Patty laughed; her friend's dramatic declarations always lifted her mood. They were sitting in the lobby of *Your Magical Wedding*, waiting for the assistant to return with some samples.

'You know, Lucy,' Patty began as she traced a finger along her chin, 'I had the strangest day a few days ago.'

Lucy smirked. 'Let me guess, does it involve a boyfriend who's too terrified to buy a ring? Or maybe the same boyfriend refusing to go to the movies because he's too tired? Because unless it does, my dear, your day can't possibly top mine.'

Patty burst into laughter again. 'I meant "strange" as in bizarre. That's everyday strange, but you'll see, soon we'll be back here planning *your* wedding. Mark my words!'

Lucy rolled her eyes, but she couldn't hide her smile.

'But seriously,' Patty continued, 'about that day … it started with a strange dream – one of those wild ones, you know? Then, on my way to work, I realised I'd forgotten my coffee at home. So, I stopped by that little café nearby.'

Lucy listened carefully.

'There was a new girl working there. She looked so overwhelmed, poor thing. Customers were being absolutely horrible to her. I don't know why, but I felt this deep sympathy for her. Like … I could see myself in her somehow.'

Lucy sighed, as though she had solved the mystery.

'Your dreams are so vivid because of all the stress you've been under lately,' Lucy started. 'Honestly, I'm surprised you even *have* dreams. If I were in your shoes, I wouldn't be able to sleep at all,' she confessed. 'First the car, then a new house, and now planning the wedding of your life … It's no wonder. And that girl? She probably reminded you of yourself a few years ago – remember when you nervously walked into our café looking for a job? We've all been there. She'll be fine. And if she can't handle the pressure, then maybe London isn't the place for her.' Lucy's face radiated satisfaction at her thorough analysis.

'Maybe you're right,' Patty said with a sigh, 'It's just … she seemed so familiar, and I can't figure out why.'

Before Lucy could respond, a cheerful voice interrupted.

'Ladies, shall we begin?

They looked up to see a young woman smartly dressed holding a folder and tablet, her badge proudly displaying *Carol – Your Wedding Planner*.

'We've never been more ready.' Lucy clapped her hands, and Patty couldn't help but laugh again.

Just a month after her first visit to the wedding agency, Patty had almost everything she needed. She had chosen a pale shade of purple as the primary player in her colour scheme, accented with a classic white for the decorations. The guest invitations and rings were also decided on. Although there was more to do, the process had been surprisingly smooth thanks to her wedding planner, Carol.

Patty and Martin hadn't wanted to delay the wedding more than they had to, setting a date in mid-September. This gave them only three months to prepare, a timeline Carol initially called ambitious, if not impossible. Yet, to everyone's surprise, everything was falling into place.

*

It was a late afternoon, and Patty was driving home after work. As she entered the neighbourhood, she passed the café where she had previously bought coffee and met the girl who seemed so intriguingly familiar. Patty had promised herself she would return to the café, but life had been so hectic that she hadn't had a chance. Even now, she was exhausted and eager to go home, have dinner with her fiancé, and discuss wedding details. But her curiosity got the better of her.

Instead of turning towards her house, she continued to the roundabout and looped back towards the café. 'It won't take long,' she thought. 'Just a quick tea.'

The place wasn't busy, so there was no need to wait in line. A young boy behind the counter, his apron hanging loosely and his face dotted with acne, was rearranging the food display. He looked up and greeted her.

'Hello! How can I help?'

'Just a mint tea, please,' Patty replied with a polite smile, though she couldn't hide her disappointment at not seeing the girl who had drawn her back.

'Anything else for you?' the boy asked after punching in the order.

'No, that'll be all, thank you,' Patty replied in turn. 'Actually, what time do you close?'

'8:00 PM, ma'am. But don't worry – you've got plenty of time for tea,' he said cheerfully.

Patty paid, carefully carried the tray with the teapot to a nearby table, and settled in. As she poured the tea, she pulled her phone from her purse and typed a quick message to Martin:

'Darling, I'll be a little late, but I'll make it on time for dinner. Love you.'

She had just sent the message when a loud clatter made her look up. A man sitting at a nearby table had accidentally knocked over a mug of hot chocolate, creating a sticky puddle on the floor that had splattered the length of several tables.

'Betty,' the boy behind the counter called loudly, 'I need you with the mop and bucket!'

Patty's heart leapt. She couldn't remember the girl's name, though she had glanced at the badge when she had placed her order, but everything happened so quickly.

A young girl came out from the kitchen, blonde hair tied in a messy ponytail; she looked to have barely been out of high school. Her shirt sleeves were rolled up to her elbows, revealing her delicate arms. She wasn't particularly tall, but her slim figure and striking features caught Patty's attention immediately. The girl's tired eyes and set jaw betrayed her exhaustion, but there was a quiet resilience about her.

Most importantly, this was *her* – the girl Patty had been hoping to see.

Betty wiped up the spilt chocolate unaware that the man who had spilt it was staring at her. Patty frowned. He was far too old for her, and the way he looked at her made Patty uncomfortable. She wanted to stand up and tell him to go home to his wife and children – who surely existed, even if he had conveniently forgotten them at that moment.

Once Betty had cleaned the mess, she returned to the kitchen. Patty sipped her tea as her mind raced. Where had she seen this girl before? A few minutes later a soft voice interrupted her thoughts.

'Excuse me, are you done with your tea?'

Patty looked up to find Betty standing in front of her, holding a tray.

'Oh, yes, of course,' she said automatically. Her mind desperately searched for a way to start a conversation. 'Are you new here?'

'Yes,' Betty replied in a friendly tone. 'I've been working here for three months.'

Encouraged, Patty smiled and continued. 'Do you like it?'

Betty laughed. 'Oh, yes. It's my dream job.'

Both of them chuckled at the obvious joke.

'I don't really have a choice right now,' Betty added. 'I just moved here and took the first job I could get. I hope it won't last forever.'

'You know,' Patty said with a soft smile as her thoughts wandered back to her own past, 'that sounds a lot like my story.'

'Really?' Betty asked, and her intrigue encouraged Patty further.

'Yes, I'm not originally from England either, but it's become my home over the years. When I first arrived, I had nothing. I started out working in a café, just like you. Day after day, I worked hard until I was ready for the next step. Don't worry – you'll find your way soon enough.'

Betty sighed. It felt like something between hope and fatigue.

'I hope so.' She glanced towards the counter. 'I should get back to work, but it was nice talking to you.'

'I'm sorry if I held you up,' Patty said quickly. Then before she could overthink it, she added, 'What if we met for coffee sometime? I'd love to talk more with you – maybe share some tips and tricks.'

Patty wasn't usually impulsive, but this felt important.

To her surprise, Betty smiled warmly. 'I'd really like that. I'm working mornings this weekend, so I'm free in the afternoons. We could meet here? One at the afternoon on Sunday?'

'In the afternoon,' Patty said with a smile and a wink.

'Right! *In*.' Betty laughed.

'I'll see you soon, then!'

Betty nodded, picked up the tray, and disappeared into the kitchen.

Patty glanced at her watch and gasped. 'I'm late!' She grabbed her purse and hurried out the door.

Despite her rush, Patty couldn't stop smiling. Beneath her chest, there was a warm bubble forming, as if she had just reconnected with an old, dear friend.

The week passed almost imperceptibly, as time often does when there seems to be too much of it for everything – except sleep. Almost every day after work, Patty found herself on the phone with her wedding planner, keeping tabs on what had been checked off the list. The weekend ahead promised to be one of the most exciting moments of the wedding preparations – choosing the wedding dress. Lucy, the most enthused maid of honour that there could ever be, had cleared her entire schedule so she could devote herself to the special task. In truth, Lucy seemed more impatient about the occasion than the bride herself. Patty had a strong feeling her best friend would be trying on dresses before her.

Saturday morning arrived with grey skies, but they couldn't touch Patty's good mood. She sang along to the radio as she drove to the bridal shop, fingers drumming in rhythm on the steering wheel. When she arrived at the dress shop, she found, with no surprise, that Lucy was already there.

'How is the most beautiful bride-to-be?' Lucy exclaimed, pulling Patty into a tight hug.

'Nervous? Can I say that?' Patty admitted with a small smile.

'Why? Everything has been going perfectly so far! You've got nothing to worry about.'

'Unless, of course, I can't find the right dress, or it doesn't fit, or they can't alter it in time … or something else goes wrong at the last moment!' Patty said in one breath.

'Okay, *almost* nothing to worry about,' Lucy corrected herself with a chuckle. 'It's going to be fine! Deep breath. You don't have *that* many reasons for anxiety. Let's start with going in.' Lucy caught her hand and led the way.

The saleswoman who greeted them warmly led them to the lobby to discuss everything before they began choosing.

'I'm looking for something simple but stylish,' Patty began, but Lucy quickly interrupted her.

'She always goes for the simple stuff, but this is a wedding! It's supposed to be magnificent!' she declared.

Patty rolled her eyes; she'd heard this argument a hundred times before, but it was impossible to get angry with Lucy here – she was like a child in a candy store. Patty wouldn't let herself break Lucy's joy, so she gave her some freedom to enjoy the moment, letting her talk as much as she needed to feel good.

'How about we start with something classic?' the saleswoman smiled. 'A big white dress with layers and a veil so we can rule it out as an option if it's really not to your taste, and in the meantime, I'll prepare some simpler options.'

'Perfect!' Lucy burst out before catching herself. 'I mean, doesn't that sound lovely, Patty?'

They both laughed and followed the saleswoman to the fitting rooms. A moment later, Patty returned wearing a dress that shifted her mood from nervous to scared.

'The perfect dress!' Lucy exclaimed, clapping her hands over her mouth.

'Actually …' Patty looked for something to say that wouldn't hurt her friend's feelings. 'Why don't you try it on? It'll be fun to see us both in white.'

'Yes!' Lucy practically ran into the fitting room.

Patty helped her get into the dress, knowing Lucy's impatience would likely lead to ripping something off accidentally.

'What do you think about picking out my maid of honour outfit tomorrow?' Lucy asked, breathing in while Patty tightened the corset.

'Maybe next weekend?' Patty said hesitantly, biting her lip.

'Busy tomorrow?'

'I have plans to meet someone,' Patty replied casually, hoping to avoid more questions. She didn't want to get into her inexplicable connection with the girl from the café. She wanted to understand it herself before sharing it with anyone else.

'Do I know this someone?' Lucy continued asking.

'I mentioned her once – a girl I ran into at the café. She seemed familiar, but when we talked, it turned out we'd never met. She's sweet, and we decided to meet for a coffee.' Patty explained, hoping this would satisfy her friend's curiosity.

'You're meeting a stranger because she *seems* familiar?' Lucy raised a sceptical eyebrow.

Before Patty could respond, the conversation shifted as Lucy caught sight of herself in the mirror and gasped.

'Oh, Lucy! You look stunning,' Patty said as her eyes went misty.

'I know, right? It's so perfect. If stupid Ben doesn't propose soon, he'll regret it forever. Should I take a photo and send it to him?'

'Sure – if you want to scare him into never proposing!' Patty teased.

Patty woke up the following day with an unusual amount of excitement about her upcoming meeting. She couldn't quite explain it, but there was something about Betty that stirred a strange sense of anticipation. Patty decided not to overthink it – her mind was already overloaded with the wedding preparations. Instead, she went to the kitchen determined to spoil her future husband with a special breakfast.

When Martin joined her half an hour later, a plate of pancakes was waiting for him. The childlike joy on his face made Patty smile – it reminded her of the old saying: 'The way to a man's heart is through his stomach.' She rested her chin in her hand as she watched him lick jam off his fingers.

'Won't you have some?' he asked with mouth half-full.

'No, love. I have to stay in shape for the wedding,' she joked.

'You don't need to,' he frowned. Then, playfully suspicious, he added, 'Seems like someone has a case of pre-wedding fever.'

'I can assure you that I suffer only from wedding impatience.' She smiled lovingly at him. 'Anyway, I don't have time to sit around. I need to get ready and head out.'

'Meeting Lucy again for wedding stuff?'

'Actually, no,' she said, realising she'd forgotten to fill him in. 'Do you remember the girl I'd mentioned, from the café?'

Martin nodded, chewing thoughtfully.

'Well, I ran into her again. She's new in town and seems really nice. I thought I'd show her around, maybe help her settle in.'

'Why are you so invested in someone you barely know? She could be trouble.' Martin raised an eyebrow.

'Trouble, Martin? I highly doubt she's trouble,' Patty jabbed.

'Okay, fair, fair, but won't it be awkward?'

'I don't think so. I can't explain it, but I just feel like she's someone worth knowing.'

'Just be careful,' he advised gently.

Patty leaned over to kiss him.

*

Betty stood in front of the café with her backpack slung over her shoulder and arms crossed. When Patty pulled up and lowered the window, she waved enthusiastically.

'Come on, hop in,' Patty called out.

Betty's face lit up with a wide smile as she climbed into the car.

'I know a great Italian restaurant. How does that sound?' Patty asked.

'Perfect,' Betty replied. 'Do you like Italian food?'

'Who doesn't? It's like I was born loving it.'

Betty chuckled. 'Same here. Though for me, it wasn't much of a choice – I grew up in Italy.'

It was a short drive to a small but cosy restaurant where Patty swore they had the best chef in town. Despite the Sunday rush, the hostess managed to seat them at a nice table. They placed their orders, laughing again when they discovered they shared the same favourite dish.

'So, Betty,' Patty said casually, 'tell me about yourself?'

Betty shrugged as if apologising in advance for disappointing. 'There's not much to tell. I grew up in a very small town.'

'Tell me about it!' Patty's eyes lit up. 'I'm in love with Italian culture. My dream is to visit someday, to wander the ancient streets and soak up all that history. It must be magical.'

Betty smiled. 'You've never been?'

'No'—Patty shook her head—'but my fiancé promised we'd go. I've even dreamt about being there.'

'Maybe he'll plan your honeymoon trip there,' Betty suggested.

Patty blinked, realising she hadn't even thought of that. It seemed so obvious now.

'You're absolutely right! And if he hasn't planned it yet, I'll make sure to suggest it.'

They both laughed.

'For someone who hasn't been there, you seem so drawn to Italy,' Betty observed. 'I'm sure it'll exceed your expectations. It's so much more than just pizza, pasta and coffee.'

'I can't even explain it,' Patty admitted, her voice getting emotional despite herself. 'It feels like an invisible force is pulling me there, like my heart knows it's home, or a second home or something …' she trailed off, suddenly self-conscious.

Betty stared at her in silence for a moment, but Patty quickly continued the conversation.

'Anyway, what made you leave Italy and come here?'

Betty blinked, as if pulling herself out of deep thought. 'I'm very attached to my country, but …' she hesitated, searching for the right words. 'Like you, something drew me away – a strange feeling, like I'm searching for something. Or someone …' She looked down, as though regretting having revealed so much.

Patty nodded, sensing there was more to Betty's story, but she didn't press. Instead, she offered a warm smile.

'Well, I'm glad your search brought you here.' After a brief pause, Patty added, 'It must be hard for your parents, being so far away from you. How did they take it?'

She tried to imagine what it might be like to one day have her own child and face a separation of that sort. Although Betty wasn't a child but a young woman, capable of making her own choices, the idea still gave Patty a heavy feeling for an inexplicable reason. Her 'sixth sense', as she called it, stirred uneasily in her chest.

Betty let out a nervous laugh, and Patty tried to shake off the strange thoughts that had taken hold of her.

'My parents … Well, I suppose they're suffering in their own way,' Betty said, 'but it was my decision to make, and they didn't have the final say.'

The waiter arrived with their plates, cutting the conversation short. Betty and Patty shifted their focus to the delicious food, and for the next hour, they moved from topic to topic as though all the time in the world wouldn't be enough to share everything they had to say.

Eventually, Patty glanced at her watch and groaned softly. 'I've had such a great time, but my fiancé's waiting for me.'

'No problem at all,' Betty replied with a bright smile. 'We should do this again soon.'

'Absolutely!' Patty not only liked the idea, she felt impatient for their next meeting. 'We'll keep in touch and plan another lunch soon.'

Outside the restaurant, Patty offered Betty a ride, but she declined, explaining she wanted to do some shopping. They hugged goodbye and exchanged numbers, promising to meet again soon.

As Patty drove home, she couldn't shake the feeling that there was something special about Betty – an invisible thread seemed to connect them. Maybe it was too early to understand the mystery around this girl, but she knew for sure this was only the beginning of a new friendship, one that would somehow change her life.

*

Patty found Martin on the couch, whistling along to a music program on TV.

'I'll never understand why I can't convince you to audition for one of those music contests,' she teased, leaning in to kiss him.

'Trust me, it'd be a disaster – for the show and for me,' he laughed, reaching for the remote to switch off the television. Then he pulled Patty into his lap and wrapped his arms around her.

'It's a shame, though,' she said playfully. 'You love music so much.'

'Loving music doesn't make me a musician,' he replied with a shrug. 'But here's a thought – next life, I'm coming back with talent. I'll conquer the world with my music.' He winked, making her laugh.

Martin reached for the small drawer in the side table and pulled out an envelope. He handed it to Patty, who looked at him curiously.

'What's this?'

'Open it, and you'll see.' His smile betrayed his excitement.

Patty tore open the envelope eagerly.

'What exactly am I looking at?'

'These,' Martin said, 'are our honeymoon tickets. A day after the wedding, we're going to Italy.'

Patty gasped as though she'd touched something too hot.

'Are you … not happy? I thought this was what you wanted,' Martin said.

'Are you kidding? Of course I'm happy! I can't believe it – we're going to Italy!'

Obviously relieved, Martin chuckled. 'For a second there, I thought I'd gotten it wrong – especially after you told me about that dream you had.'

'No, you got it absolutely right! I'm just stunned – it's such an interesting coincidence. Betty, the friend I had lunch with today, just suggested you might surprise me with a honeymoon in Italy. Isn't that wild? She's Italian, by the way. It feels like everything around me lately is connected to Italy.'

Martin raised an eyebrow. 'That's quite the coincidence ... Maybe it's time you introduced me to your new friend. You've been talking about her nonstop. And don't make Lucy jealous – she can be dangerous,' he teased, making Patty laugh again.

'You're right. I'll introduce her to everyone soon – she's the sweetest girl, impossible not to like. But now, I need to call Lucy and tell her about the honeymoon!'

That night, Patty had another strange dream. Reality, fantasy, and memories all seemed to merge into one. Once again, she was in a version of Italy long gone. Betty was there, too, by her side. Lucy appeared, helping her get dressed, and later, Martin joined the scene with a musical instrument in hand. He came over and kissed her passionately ...

*

It was less than a month until the wedding day. Everything was going as planned; the tension was manageable, happiness was bubbling over, and something new was blossoming. Despite her busy schedule, torn between work and wedding preparations, Patty made time for her friendship with Betty.

The doorbell rang, and Martin walked over to answer it while Lucy and Patty were setting the table, discussing details around the wedding as usual.

'Hello,' he greeted with a warm smile. 'You must be Betty.'

Betty stood on the doorstep, nervous, holding a bottle of wine in her hand.

'Nice to meet you,' she said, smiling and stretching out her free hand.

'And you,' Martin replied, shaking her hand. 'Come on in. Let me take your jacket.'

'Thank you. Oh, and … this is for you,' she said, handing him the bottle.

'Very kind of you, but you didn't have to,' Martin replied, accepting the wine as he helped her out of her jacket.

Betty was worried, even more than she'd expected to be. Stepping into the home of the woman she secretly thought of as her 'long-lost mother' made her chest tighten with both excitement and fear. Being welcomed into Patty's life, meeting her closest friends, and feeling like part of her inner circle was more than she had dared to hope for. And yet, she knew she couldn't reveal the truth. What if Patty thought Betty was crazy and rejected her forever?

'This way,' Martin said, gesturing towards the living room.

As they entered, Patty jumped up from her seat with a shout of joy. She rushed to Betty and hugged her warmly.

'Betty! I'm so glad you're here,' she said. 'Let me introduce you to my best friend Lucy, and her boyfriend Ben.'

Lucy had teased Patty earlier about this mysterious new friend who had suddenly taken her attention, but when she saw Betty, something shifted. A strange warmth filled her chest. Instead of simply shaking hands, Lucy hugged Betty and kissed her on the cheek.

Betty's nerves melted away. The warmth of the welcome she received made her feel less like a stranger in a foreign country and more like a long-lost family member coming home.

'It was so thoughtful of her to bring a bottle of wine,' Martin said.

'It's an Italian wine from the region where I grew up,' Betty explained.

Patty clapped her hands joyfully. 'Perfect! Let's open it and enjoy it in the garden while we wait for the food to be ready.'

Everyone agreed enthusiastically and made their way through the glass doors to the garden. The evening was full of lively conversation and laughter. For the first time in what felt like forever, Betty didn't miss home, family, or friends. She was simply happy.

At one point, Betty and Patty found themselves alone in the garden for a moment. 'You know,' Patty began with a thoughtful tone, 'we haven't known each other for long, but I feel like I've already gotten a good sense of who you are.'

Betty's heart raced. She wanted so badly to express what this connection meant to her without scaring Patty away.

'I feel the same way,' she said with a nervous smile. 'Honestly, it feels like we're friends who've found each other again, rather than just starting something new.'

Patty's gaze drifted somewhere into the darkness of the garden, and Betty bit her lip, afraid she had said too much. But then Patty spoke again.

'Strangely enough, I would describe it the exact same way.'

'I'm glad,' Betty said softly.

'That's why I thought it was only right to give you this.' Patty pulled a small envelope from the pocket of her jacket. She handed it to Betty with a smile.

'What's this?'

'Open it,' Patty urged.

Inside, Betty found a luxurious sheet of paper with elegant writing. She read the words aloud.

You're invited to the Wedding of Martin and Patricia.

Betty's eyes widened. 'Really?'

'Yes,' Patty said firmly. 'I want you to be part of the most important day of my life.'

Overwhelmed, Betty embraced Patty, as no words would do.

*

September 18th. The sun was just beginning to break through the soft clouds, offering a gentle warmth. The slight breeze had just enough bite to make someone reach for a jacket.

Most importantly, it was *the big day* – Patty and Martin's wedding.

Patty woke up at 6:00 am on the dot, as scheduled, but not in great shape. She hadn't slept the night before, which although understandable, didn't help.

Following tradition, she and Martin were getting ready separately, so Patty planned to head over to Lucy's house, where Lucy and Betty would help her with hair and makeup. Everything was perfectly organised, yet all the preparation in the world couldn't help with the feeling in her stomach. As soon as she got out of bed, she rushed to the bathroom. Turning on the cold water, she leaned over the sink, letting the sound and feel of the running water soothe her nerves. After a few moments, she felt better.

It must be the pressure, she thought as she splashed cold water on her face and straightened up.

She quickly dressed and headed to the kitchen, where Martin was sitting at the table, picking at a muffin that was barely touched.

His stomach must be in knots, too.

She approached him, brushing her hand tenderly across his cheek. He smiled, but his eyes revealed he hadn't slept much, either.

'I'll see you later,' she said, leaning in to kiss him. 'Our last kiss as fiancés.'

'Yeah,' he replied with a nervous laugh. 'The next kiss will be in front of our parents and at least forty other people.'

Patty winked and grabbed her purse.

'Hey,' Martin called out as she reached the door, 'I'll be the guy in the black suit standing in front of the altar.'

She laughed and the door clicked shut behind her.

At Lucy's house, the mood was light and playful, almost like they were getting ready for a girls' night out. Hair straighteners and makeup palettes were being passed around while their dresses hung neatly on the wardrobe – safe from Lucy's curious cat. Time seemed to fly by, and before they knew it, the clock showed 11:00 am. With the ceremony scheduled for noon, they had to pick up the pace.

'You are the most beautiful bride,' Lucy squeaked, tears threatening to fall as Patty looked at herself in the mirror one last time.

'I think we're all going to ruin our makeup before the ceremony even starts,' Betty added, moved by the moment as well.

Patty smiled, wiping the corners of her eyes. 'No tears until after the vows, okay?'

They laughed together and Patty suddenly placed a hand over her stomach.

'Oh, not again …' she muttered, closing her eyes and breathing steadily in hopes that the sensation would soon fade.

'What's wrong?' Lucy and Betty circled her, taking her arms to steady her in case she fainted.

'It's just the stress – nothing serious,' Patty said quietly. 'I felt sick this morning, and now it's happening again … I just hope it doesn't happen during the ceremony.'

'If it weren't for all the wedding excitement, I'd have thought you were pregnant,' Lucy said casually.

Patty turned to her abruptly, her eyes were now wide with a mixture of shock and disbelief. The tension on her face revealed just how possible yet utterly overwhelming that idea was to her, especially on her wedding day.

'It can't be true,' she whispered, mostly to herself. Even as she said it, her voice trembled, betraying the seed of doubt that had already taken root in her mind.

'Honestly, it wouldn't be *that* surprising,' Betty commented.

A heavy silence fell over the room, broken only by the soft purring of Lucy's cat.

'I think you should take a test,' Betty suggested gently. 'Just to calm yourself down … if it's negative.'

'And if it's positive?' Patty asked breathlessly, feeling the blood draining from her face.

'Honey, listen to me.' Lucy stepped in with the voice of authority. 'There is no reason for panic. This is just a guess. But, as Betty suggested, it's best to confirm – just to be sure.'

Patty only nodded – too stunned to speak. Lucy disappeared for a moment and returned holding something out to Patty.

'Take this to the bathroom and let's get this over with. We *really* need to leave soon, and you cannot be late to your own wedding!'

'You just had one of these lying around?' Patty asked.

'I like to have one on hand – now's not the time for questions.'

Patty obeyed. She could hear her two friends pacing nervously in the other room. When she returned a few minutes later, she held the test in her hand.

'For the record, peeing on a stick while wearing a wedding dress is *not* easy.'

Lucy and Betty burst into nervous laughter.

'We don't have time to wait for the result. Let's jump in the car; we'll check it on the way.'

'No!' Patty protested. 'I don't want to know before the wedding. It'll distract me and make me even more nervous.' She paused, trying to think of a solution. 'That's why, Betty, I'm giving it to you. You'll tell me the result *after* the ceremony.'

She handed the test to Betty, whose wide eyes revealed the weight of the responsibility that had just been thrust upon her. Quickly pulling herself together, she slipped the test into her purse.

They headed for the car and set off. The journey wasn't long, but Betty felt her curiosity growing by the second. She resisted the overwhelming urge to peek into her purse, knowing that if she did, her reaction – no matter how subtle – would betray her. Biting her lip, she kept her hands away from her purse.

The car pulled up in front of the venue, a beautiful house transformed into a wedding wonderland. Betty had attended only a handful of weddings in her life, but this was by far the most enchanting.

'This is it – my big moment.' Patty grinned.

Patty's father appeared, with tears in his eyes as he embraced his daughter. Maggie, Patty's younger sister and fellow bridesmaid, joined them, and Betty immediately got on with her.

The music began. Betty and Maggie stepped forwards with baskets of colourful petals in hand. As Betty approached the altar and branched off to take her seat, she couldn't help but think about the secret tucked inside her purse. In the brief moment as everyone awaited the bride's appearance, she gave in to temptation. Pulling the test from her bag, she glanced at it quickly.

Two unmistakable red lines.

The murmurs of the guests made Betty look up, and there was Patty, radiant, floating down the aisle. With her father by her side, and Lucy, her maid of honour, following behind, Patty met Betty's gaze and smiled softly.

Everyone Betty loved was now in her life.

THE

END

ACKNOWLEDGMENTS

I will forever remember the day I first sat down to write this book. With a notebook in hand, I carefully mapped out the entire story from start to finish – the whole idea was so vivid in my mind. Having a clear vision and a detailed plan felt like the perfect start. I was excited, hopeful, and confident. Now, eight years later, after facing every possible obstacle, as this book finally comes to life, I realise how naïve I once was and how much this journey has changed me.

Despite the many challenges along the way, I'm deeply grateful for everything that brought me to this moment. The first and most heartfelt thank you goes to Angel, who is sadly no longer with us. Without his encouragement, I might never have sat down to write this book in the first place. I'm also endlessly grateful to the people closest to me for their support – believing in me, especially in moments I doubted myself, meant more than words can express. A huge thank you to my editor Phoenix Raig, for his thoughtful insights and dedication to refining this story. Many thanks to PublishNation for assisting me with the self-publishing process for each of my books. There are no words to describe how it feels to finally see this dream project become a reality.

This book features many well-known and widely recognised quotes, along with some lesser-known ones, including those from Bulgarian poets and writers. I felt it was important to include them as a tribute to my heritage and roots.

And lastly, I want to thank myself – for pushing through, and for learning the difficult but invaluable lesson of never giving up. It wasn't easy, but every challenge, every setback, and every tear was worth it.

About the Author

Lora Kay is a self-published author. Born and raised in Bulgaria, she later moved to the United Kingdom, where she studied Psychology at the University of West London. She balances her time between working and writing, pursuing her passion for storytelling.

Lora finds great joy in creating manuscripts that explore the complexities of human emotions. Her stories often carry a darker tone, offering a lens into the raw and unfiltered aspects of life. Her love for books has always been a driving force – not just as a reader, but as a writer committed to exploring themes that spark reflection and raise awareness of important issues.

Her books are available worldwide.

Connect with Lora on Instagram
@lora_kay_writer.